Olin woke to a thunde[...] [...]led up from his cot and tried to get his bearings. "Who's there?"

Seeing nothing, he slipped on his boots and worked his way to the front of the smithy. Opening the barn door allowed full light to flow into the area. Seeing nothing out of place, he ran around the corner of the building to Ida Mae's front door.

The iron handle wouldn't move. "Locked." He rattled the door in its hinges. "Ida Mae!"

The sign in the window said Closed. He didn't like it. He ran back to his shop and picked up the tools he needed to force entry. That's when he spotted the window. How had he missed it? Framed by shattered glass, Ida Mae stood looking out toward him. "Let me in, lass."

She stood for a moment looking past him, then shook her head slightly and walked toward the door.

He slipped through and had her in his arms before she'd fully opened the door. "Are ye all right?"

The blue in her eyes darkened. She said nothing. He held her closer and whispered in her ear. "You're safe now."

He swept her up into his arms and carried her over to the area where the rock had been tossed. This rock was much larger than the one before. Carrying her to the back room, he gently set her on the chair. "I'll be right back."

She nodded, but not a word came from her lips.

He pulled himself away and went to the rock. A note was wrapped around this one, as well. He untied it and read the ugly message. A horrible word he couldn't even repeat blazed across the crumpled paper.

LYNN A. COLEMAN was raised on Martha's Vineyard and now calls Florida home. She has three grown children and eight grandchildren. She is a minister's wife who writes to the Lord's glory. She served as advisor of the American Christian Romance Writers Inc. Lynn enjoys hearing from her readers. Visit her Web page at www.lynncoleman.com.

Books by Lynn A. Coleman

HEARTSONG PRESENTS

Don't miss out on any of our super romances. Write to us at the following address for information on our newest releases and club information.

Heartsong Presents Readers' Service
PO Box 721
Uhrichsville, OH 44683

Or visit www.heartsongpresents.com

Corduroy
Road to Love

Lynn A. Coleman

Heartsong Presents

To my son, Tim, and his wife, Farrah—the newest member of the family.

A note from the Author:
I love to hear from my readers! You may correspond with me by writing:

Lynn A. Coleman
Author Relations
PO Box 721
Uhrichsville, OH 44683

ISBN 978-1-59789-646-7

CORDUROY ROAD TO LOVE

Scripture quotations are taken from the King James Version of the Bible.

All of the characters and events in this book are fictitious. Any resemblance to actual persons, living or dead, or to actual events is purely coincidental.

Our mission is to publish and distribute inspirational products offering exceptional value and biblical encouragement to the masses.

PRINTED IN THE U.S.A.

one

1830
Charlotte, North Carolina

"Ida Mae, I can't believe you're renting the barn to a tinker. I daresay, isn't he a week late?"

"Minnie, I told you he's a tinsmith, not a tinker."

"Tinsmith, tinker—doesn't matter, he's a stranger. He's not one of us, Ida Mae, and you ought to know better. With the way your pa and ma. . . Well, mark my words, it ain't right, you letting a stranger move in so close to ya. Unless you're re-considering Cyrus's offer."

Ida Mae loved her cousin, but sometimes the woman could really tangle her threads. "No, I'm not going to marry Cyrus Morgan. He's a kind man, but the Lord and I have an understanding."

Minnie's brown hair swayed back and forth as she shook her head. "Ain't no man going to fill that understandin', as you say. Only one that could is the good Lord Himself, and He chose not to marry when He was on this here earth. So I say you're aiming to be a spinster, in both meanings of the word."

Ida Mae often thought it odd that her profession was also the name for an old woman who never married. And it seemed odd that Minnie, who was nearly the same age as herself, would feel the need to inform her on the ways of man, courtship, and marriage. Ida Mae sat back down and started spinning the flax into threads. Tomorrow she'd have to get to work on the wool brought in by John Alexander Farres. Folks used John's middle name to help distinguish him from the various cousins in the area. Not that she should have a problem with that, since she answered to her first two names.

5

"I give up." Minnie stomped out the front door and headed across the street.

Ida Mae closed her eyes and prayed she hadn't offended her cousin again. Minnie and the rest of the family meant well, but it seemed ever since her parents died last year, everyone thought they had a right to tell her what to do. Ida Mae blew a strand of blond hair from her face. The order of flax needed to be spun before she could begin work on the woolen yarn for the Farreses. Mama used to weave the linen threads into fine cloth, but Ida Mae didn't have the same hand. The woven cloth was adequate and could be used for work clothing and such, but it wasn't the kind of fabric that could grace the tables of elegant homes.

Cyrus had been mighty helpful after the fire that had killed her parents and destroyed their home last year. He had single-handedly performed most of the reconstruction. But she couldn't marry him. She didn't love him, not like the Bible talked about in the Song of Songs. *Cyrus is a good man but. . . I don't know, Lord, is there something wrong with me? Am I made like the apostle Paul and meant to be single all my life?*

A wagon full of wares pulled up outside the storefront that had been doubling as her living quarters for the past year.

A man with an odd-shaped hat jumped down and secured his horse. He marched up the steps right to her open front door. "Good day, would you be Miss McAuley?"

"Yes, sir."

He swooped off his odd cap, revealing a healthy crop of black hair, and bowed slightly. "Pleasure to make yer acquaintance, Miss. I'm Olin Orr. I believe you've been expecting me."

Ida Mae tightened her jaw to make certain she hadn't dropped it. No man had ever bowed to her before. Folks around these parts weren't lacking formal manners—they just didn't have much use for them. Not like Mr. Olin Orr from the big city of Philadelphia, Pennsylvania. His hair was a mixture of silk and dark walnut, and curls that a woman's fingers could have fun— Ida Mae quelled her foolish thoughts. "Yes, your post said you'd be arriving last week."

"Aye. I'm afraid I misspoke in my correspondence. The roads were far worse than I recalled them. I often had to make or repair some corduroy roads in order to pass with my wagon. Springtime brings many showers and the creeks are up."

"I see." She could well imagine how many trees he'd had to cut down to get over those muddy holes. But she wondered if he was the type of man to place the logs securely over the road for the next passerby. She glanced at his wagon in front of her shop; even riding over the felled logs, it must have been difficult because of the constant bumps, so like corduroy fabric. In fact, she should fell some trees on the road leading up to the family homestead, but she didn't see much point since she wasn't using it. "Let me show you the barn. I hope it is what you were expecting. I tried to be honest and fair with our dealings, Mr. Orr."

"Aye, more than fair, Miss McAuley."

Ida Mae nodded and headed out the front door. She locked it, then gestured to her right and walked north toward the end of the building. Mr. Orr followed close behind but left a distance of several feet between them until rounding the corner and stopping at the door to the smithy. Father's blacksmith shop was a stable that he had converted. It seemed the perfect place for a tinsmith. But she had hoped the man would want to blacksmith. Too many folks had high dreams of finding gold like the members of the Reed family had found on their property thirty years ago. The Reed farm was a gold mine now, and word around town was they were talking about digging tunnels to remove ore from the quartz rock below, unlike the way they had been mining. Gold had been found on various farms all over the area. The way folks were moving into the area, you'd think they were just fortune seekers.

"What brings you to Charlotte, Mr. Orr?" She slid the large board to the right to open the barn door.

"Work," he answered. That, she already knew. For a man who could toss out some fancy words, he sure seemed quiet when it came to details about his personal life.

Slivers of sunlight poured into the old shop. Ida Mae hadn't stepped foot in here since her father's death. A knot in her stomach threatened to squeeze the tears right out of her. She cleared her throat. "I'll let you have a look around. I'll meet you back in the store."

"Thank ye, Miss." He plopped that odd hat back on his head and stepped inside.

Ida Mae couldn't face the memories of her father and hustled back to her shop. Quickly setting her hands to the wheel and her foot to the pedal, she began spinning the flax once again.

❧

To do his tinwork, Olin didn't need the equipment that the blacksmith had used. But the additional income from making horseshoes and such was worth keeping the equipment in place. The shop had a year's worth of dust and grit all over the tables and equipment. His parents had written and told him of the tragedy that had befallen Thomas McAuley and his wife. It seemed odd that a man who worked with fire would die by it in his home. He'd heard of blacksmiths dying in accidents relating to their work—but that was between Mr. McAuley and his Maker.

Stepping back into the open doorway, he looked over the town. It had changed in the past seven years he'd been gone. Olin wondered how many would remember what happened before he left. He had been seventeen at the time and full of himself. *Should I have stayed away, Lord?*

Thankfully, Ida Mae didn't remember him. Not that she would, he supposed. She was two years younger. And by the time she was twelve she had stopped going to the church school to work full-time with her parents. They were an older couple. She was ten years younger than her brothers, who had all moved away with the promise of larger amounts of land in the frontier.

He would have gone west if his father hadn't intervened

and set him up in the apprenticeship. He slapped the dust from his hat and gave the barn one final glance. Taking a determined step forward, he headed back into the store.

"Mr. Orr, is it satisfactory?"

"Aye, Miss. I'll bring in the twenty-five dollars after I visit with the bank tomorrow. Is it all right if I begin moving my belongings in now, or would you prefer I wait until a lease has been signed?"

"Beggin' your pardon, Mr. Orr. I'm afraid I should wait until the papers and money have been exchanged."

Olin nodded. He would have done the same if a stranger had asked him. "You're a fine businesswoman. I'll see ye on the morrow. God's blessing to you."

He strode up to the wagon and checked his horse before pushing on the extra thirty minutes to his parents' farm. He would have preferred to leave the wagon in the barn to lessen the horse's burden. On the other hand, he had a few gifts for his family stowed in the wagon. The animal needed a good grooming and a comfortable stall to sleep in. Ida Mae McAuley's barn had room for one horse. The loft would make a suitable place for him to live until his business was established enough to provide sufficient income to support himself. Mother would make sure he had enough to eat. He'd been sending money home for years, but he'd also had few expenses in Pennsylvania. The closer he came to the old farm, the more memories swarmed around like a stirred-up hornet's nest. He supposed it only seemed fitting since the area had a reputation of being a hornet's nest from the Revolutionary War.

One of the things that seemed different was passing slaves working on a large plantation just outside the city. Years ago that property had belonged to three different yeoman farmers, like his parents. Each had lots of five hundred acres, enough to make a profit, but not so much that a man would need to hire slaves.

"Olin!" His mother ran out the door with outstretched arms. Joy erupted through his body. *Aye, it is good to be home.* He jumped down from the wagon and wrapped his mother in a bear hug. He'd missed this woman and, until this moment, hadn't realized just how much. It had been seven years. *Why didn't I come sooner?* "Mother, it's good to see ye."

She wiped her blue eyes with her apron. "Aye, it's good to see ye, son. I thought I'd never see ye again."

"I'm home, Mother. I plan on staying and living here the rest of my days."

"Well, God be praised! Then it was a good thing ye left for seven years. Now I shall see ye marry and give me lots of grandbabies."

Olin chuckled. "I had better find a wife first, Mum."

"Aye, or I would do a whole lot more than just pull your ear."

He rubbed his right ear, remembering all the times he'd been hauled off to the woodshed to be paddled by his father for misbehaving.

"Your father says you'll be living at Mr. McAuley's black-smith shop. Ye need to stay here. I won't be having ye living in no barn. No son of mine—"

"Mother, please." He cut her off. "There's plenty of time to discuss this, but let me take care of my horse. He's worked hard."

"Aye. I'll be settin' a place for ye at dinner."

"Thank ye. It's good to be home."

Fresh tears spilled from his mother's eyes. He turned as his mother left. His own eyes moistened as he unfastened the carriage from his horse. He patted the brown stallion. "I bet that feels good, boy."

Carson neighed his approval.

Olin gave the familiar *cluck*, and the horse obeyed, following him to the barn. Fresh oats, water, and some overdue grooming set the beast up for the night. Finally, Olin pumped some water into the outdoor basin and cleaned off some of the caked-on road grime.

"Well, well, it's the devil himself!"

Olin spun around.

a

"Ida Mae, Ida Mae!" Minnie came running into the shop, breathing hard. "You'll never believe this, but Mr. Orr is not a stranger. He's from around here."

Ida Mae glanced up from her spinning. *I already suspected that.* "Several Orr families live around here."

"Yes, but how many do you know are murderers?"

Murderer. Ida Mae stopped the wheel. "What are you sayin'?"

Minnie's brown eyes darted back and forth. "Rumor has it that Bobby Orr killed another miner seven years back."

"I can't be going on rumors. What are folks sayin'?"

"Well, you remember seven years back when there was some fighting going on at the Reeds' gold mine."

"There's always fights going on at the gold mines."

"Well, this one ended in a fella getting killed. A Bobby Orr was the one responsible for the man's death."

"Honestly, Minnie, I don't see what this has to do with our Mr. Orr."

"That's just it; he's the same man."

"His name is Olin. Folks must be mistaken."

Minnie tossed her head back and forth. "Nope, he's the one. I tell ya, he's the same man."

"How do you know?"

"Folks seen him, that's how. Not to mention, his own kin been tellin' folks he's comin' back, and they ain't none too happy about it neither. They say he's the devil himself. He has a temper that makes the devil run."

Ida Mae took in a deep breath and let it out slowly. She didn't care for gossip and knew Minnie could keep a person's ear full for years. *But is it true, Lord?* She had to admit, she was concerned.

"Ain't he planning on livin' in the shop? I don't mean to tell ya your business, Ida Mae, but I wouldn't be sleepin' on the same property with no killer. No sirree!"

Fear spiraled down Ida Mae's spine like a thick wool thread

spun on the spooler. She'd been putting off moving back into the farmhouse. Maybe it was time. "There must be some mistake; Mr. Orr is a perfect gentleman."

"Don't be fooled. Even the Good Book says the devil—he comes as an angel of light. I'm tellin' ya, nothin' good can come of this, Ida Mae. You best tell him to pack his bags and move on."

And wouldn't her father roll in his grave if he knew she'd treated someone so poorly, not knowing for certain if he was guilty? "If he's the one, why wasn't he arrested and hanged?"

Minnie marched back and forth with her hands on her hips. "That's the odd thing. No one seems to know. All folks can say is that he got away with murder and left. Maybe his daddy paid off the sheriff. 'Course, they never found any gold at the Orrs' farm. I don't know, Ida Mae, but it don't seem right."

"Minnie, thank you for telling me. I'll speak with Mr. Orr when it is appropriate and ask."

"I'm tellin' ya, mark my words, that man is trouble. Even his own kin ain't none too happy. This just ain't a good thing, Ida Mae."

You've already said that. "Thank you, again. Let me get back to work and finish up this order. I need to go out to the farmstead before dark."

A glint in Minnie's eyes made Ida Mae aware she'd said or done something that met with her cousin's approval. There seemed to be precious little that did since her folks died. Why Minnie had decided to become Ida Mae's self-appointed guardian, she would never know.

"I heard Cyrus was going out there this afternoon. He's planting for you."

Yes, I know that. "I might just run into him out there. What are you folks planting this year?"

"Cotton, beans, some corn. . . Same as usual. What are you an' Cyrus planting?"

Ida Mae didn't like hearing her and Cyrus's names wrapped

together in the same sentence, knowing what Minnie and others thought. "Those, plus a few other vegetables. I'm hoping to do some more canning."

"How's your peach and pecan trees coming along?" Minnie asked, and the two of them talked for the next ten minutes about farming and marketing the farm's surplus.

If only the road to the north was in better shape, Ida Mae mused. Then she remembered Olin saying how he'd repaired quite a few places along the road. *A killer wouldn't do that, would he?*

After Minnie left, Ida Mae finished the flax order and rode her horse out to the family farmstead. The peach blossoms were in full bloom, lining the road to the house. The rebuilt two-story federalist-style house was freshly painted. Cyrus did fine work. How could she ever convince him she wasn't interested in marrying him? Perhaps she *should* marry him just to ease her conscience.

Ida Mae's thoughts wandered to her childhood days as she rode up the drive. Her parents' farm was smaller than most in the area, and her father had been content with small crops, especially when demand for his blacksmith talents became more lucrative than farming. When her older brothers were able to tend the land on their own, her father bought an old barn in Charlotte and transformed the north half into a smithy and the south end into a shop for his wife's spinning wheels and loom. Her parents hadn't anticipated that the boys would head west, leaving the farm available for Ida Mae's inheritance, either to sell or to work the land with her future husband. How quickly things had changed.

As she reached the end of the drive, Cyrus's rugged, six-foot frame slipped out of the barn. He was a good enough looking man, and he was kind. He'd make a good father, she tried to convince herself. He smiled and waved.

"How ya doin', Ida Mae? I didn't expect to see you out here tonight."

The barn door creaked open.

Rosey Turner peeked around the door, her hair all mussed.

"Cyrus?" Ida Mae pointed to Rosey.

Crimson filled Cyrus's cheeks. "Uh, Rosey came to lend me a hand tonight."

two

"Percy Mandrake, what brings ye here on this fine day?"

Percy relaxed his accusatory stance and turned toward Olin's father. "Uncle Thomas. Good to see you."

Olin stretched his neck from side to side to release the tension that had filled him when Percy surprised him from behind. There never had been any love lost between him and his cousin. Each meeting tended to end in fisticuffs. Olin redirected his gaze to his father. It was good to see him. He had aged some in the last seven years but still retained his rugged stance and the square set to his shoulders.

"Aye, but we've not seen ye for pretty near a year. Is your mother all right?"

"She's fine." Percy turned toward Olin. "I heard Bobby was back in town and thought I'd pay him a visit."

"Well, that be mighty nice of ye. Your aunt has put on quite a spread. Would ye care to stay for dinner?"

Olin dried his hands on the towel kept by the pump.

"Don't mind if I do."

Give me grace, Lord. Olin placed the towel back over the pump handle. He thought about telling his cousin he went by his given name now, but what would be the use? To Percy and the rest of the clan he would always be Bobby.

"What are ye doin' these days?"

Percy narrowed his gaze and focused directly at Olin. "Been making an honest living."

Olin walked toward his father, directly past Percy. In the old days Olin would have taken Percy's words as a challenge. But today—and hopefully the rest of his days—he would continue to let negative comments pass.

"Doing what?" he asked Percy.

"Farmin'. Your mother says you're a tin man. Ain't got much use for them down in these parts. Them Yankees are cheats."

Olin had heard about the Yankee merchants who had come to the South, charging three to four times more for items than they were worth and hurting the poor area farmers. "I am a tinsmith. Came here to set up shop so folks can buy from a local."

"And I'm mighty pleased. Good to have ye home, son." His father enveloped him in a big bear hug.

"Good to be home, Pa."

Olin thought he heard Percy snicker behind him but didn't let that bother him, either. Nope. A lot of things in the past that would have given him cause to get angry just didn't seem important now.

"How was the trip? In your letters ye said you'd be home a week ago."

"The roads were in horrific shape. A lot of spring flooding. I had to spend quite a few hours repairing the stretches of corduroy roads. My wagon," Olin said as he pointed to an overburdened cart, "wouldn't make it without me fixing 'em."

His father whistled. "What's in there?"

"All my tools, plus a few things I brought from Pennsylvania to set up my living quarters."

"Your mother will persuade ye out of that."

"She'll try."

"Why would you want to live in town?" Percy looked down-right confused.

"Been living on my own for a while now. If I live at the shop, I can work late hours if I have an order that needs fixing as soon as possible."

"Ain't no one in a rush around here." Percy stepped up to the two of them.

Olin suspected that Percy still lived at home and enjoyed having his mother do his laundry, clean his room, and make his meals every day. Personally, Olin liked being on his own and felt Percy—at twenty-five years of age—ought to. Then again, folks tended to live at home until they married, and even then they'd sometimes live in their parents' house until they could build their own home on the family property. Percy's father was one who kept a tight rein on his money and land, so it was quite possible his father wouldn't give him a piece of land to build on.

Olin's older brothers, John and Kyle, came in from the fields and joined them with warm welcomes and genuine love. Percy seemed to be the only curious feature in the small family gathering. Olin's sisters were married and living with their husbands. Janet lived in the area and had several children, including a set of twins. Olin's heart tightened. He hadn't even come home for his sisters' weddings.

They went into the house and sat down at the fancy, dressed table. Mother had even pulled out her Sunday china. He felt like the prodigal son home from his years of squandering. But he hadn't been squandering his inheritance; he'd been working hard at his trade and at controlling his anger. His mentor, William Farley, had been more than a mentor of tinsmithing. He'd helped Olin heal his heart and develop his relationship with his Savior.

Percy leaned over to Kyle and whispered, "Wanna run him out of town?"

๛

Ida Mae glanced at Cyrus, then back to Rosey. *There is more going on here than Rosey just giving Cyrus a hand. Why would he ask to marry me if he was interested in Rosey? And why do I not feel offended that he might marry her?* Ida Mae knew she didn't love Cyrus but. . .why wasn't she more upset?

"Cyrus, is the house habitable?"

"Yes, it's all set."

"Good, I'll be moving back in tomorrow."

"Tomorrow?" Cyrus and Rosey said in unison.

"Is there a problem?"

"No, it's just I've been talkin' to Rosey about renting the house and farming the place for you. I was meanin' to speak with you about it next week."

Rosey put her hands on her hips. "Cyrus, you said. . ."

Cyrus's cheeks flamed scarlet red. "Rosey, honey, I meant to speak with her. I just got busy, is all."

Ida Mae sighed. She didn't want to get in the middle of a lovers' spat. And at the moment she wasn't too pleased with herself for even considering the possibility of marrying Cyrus. "Let's go inside; I want to see the work you've done."

After a fifteen-minute tour of the house, they sat down at the kitchen table Cyrus must have built. There were only three chairs, but that worked fine.

"See, Ida Mae, I was planning on asking you if I could live in the house and do the farming on the land. I'll show a profit to you every year. Unless, of course, the good Lord brings about bad weather and insects."

Every farmer knew they were dependent on the weather, rainfall, and no swarming locusts to have a good crop.

"I'll even pay ya something to rent the house, if'n ya feel it's necessary. But if Rosey and I are going to be able to save for our own farm, it will take longer."

Rosey smacked Cyrus on the arm. "Tell her all of it."

"Me and Rosey got married this morning. Family don't know yet. We're planning on keepin' it a secret for a spell."

Ida Mae rubbed the back of her neck. "You're married?"

"Yup, got the paper right here."

"Pa will explode," Rosey interrupted, "since Cyrus don't own his own land and home yet."

All the pieces came together—why the secret, why the desire to rent her property. And it solved the uncomfortable problem she had with returning to her home where her parents had died. She hadn't expected much from the land this year, what with her brothers being unable to help and their parents' estate unfinished, not to mention the house needing to be rebuilt. But now. . .

"I'll have my father's attorney draw up a lease agreement for one year. I'll pay you a percentage of the profit from the harvest, if there is a profit. I won't charge for the house, but I'll expect you to finish the barn and do upkeep on the house. How's that?"

Cyrus's smile barely curved his lips. "Sounds right nice, thank you."

"Come to town tomorrow eve and I'll have the paperwork ready to sign."

His Adam's apple bouncing up and down in his throat, Cyrus swallowed hard. Rosey beamed.

"I best be going, seeing as it's your wedding night and all." Ida Mae pushed her chair from under the table and got up to leave. Minnie would not be happy with her staying in town.

"Cyrus, can I speak with you for a moment outside?"

"Be my pleasure, Ida Mae."

Her backbone twitched just hearing his words. Memories of his latest proposal—a mere month ago— flooded back into her mind, leaving her feeling rankled. The walk out to her horse helped soothe her nerves. "You've been planning this for a while, and you didn't speak with me."

"I'm sorry, Ida Mae, I meant to. I've been so busy getting the house ready, plowing the fields, and courtin' Rosey, I just ran out of time."

"It's not sound business, Cyrus." *Not to mention, the last time we spoke you proposed marriage to me. I hope Rosey knows what she's getting into.*

"You're right. You always did have a good eye for business. Take a look at the fields I've been plowing and planting."

Scanning the fields, Ida Mae saw little done. *Father would have had it all plowed and planted by now*, she thought wistfully. "Are you planning on planting all the fields?"

"No, I felt most of the land would prosper better with a year of rest. I'm going to bring the cows and horses out in the idle fields over the summer and allow them to do their job."

Resting the land was not an uncommon practice, and since she hadn't given him any orders, or even spoken with him about the farm, it seemed a reasonable plan. Something she realized she should have considered much sooner. But farming had been far from her mind, and living on the farm once the house was rebuilt, even farther. "That will be fine, Cyrus. I'll expect to see you tomorrow eve."

"Thank you, Ida Mae. And again, I'm sorry for not speakin' with ya sooner."

"I understand." Ida Mae climbed onto her horse and sat in the saddle sideways, already regretting having made such a hasty decision.

She waved him off and headed back toward town. It would be dark before she returned and she hadn't brought a lantern with her. *Lord, there's a part of me that isn't excited about renting the house and having Cyrus farm the land for me, but honestly, I can't do it. I wasn't planning on becoming a landlord. Give me grace and the knowledge to handle all this.*

Her mind wove back to her other tenant, the murderer, if Minnie was correct. Truth was, she trusted him more than she trusted Cyrus. *Dear God, please give me wisdom.*

❧

Olin sat back in his chair. Percy left just before it was time to clear the table and do evening chores. The ring of Mother's finest silver on the china reminded him of many meals he'd eaten with his family over the years, so unlike the past seven years.

"It's good to have ye home, son. And don't ye worry none about Percy. Folks just need to gossip every now and again. Once you've been living here for a while, things will get better. Won't they, Kyle?"

Kyle forked the last potato chunk from his plate. "Yes, sir. And after ye were gone, folks were pretty divided about who started that fight. Everyone that was at the fight acknowledged it wasn't your fault."

Olin nodded.

"Bobby, why'd ye come back?" his oldest brother, John, asked.

"Mum wrote about the Yankee traders selling tinware in the area and how so many folks paid too much for them. I'm fairly good at the trade and thought folks would like to buy tin made from someone who grew up here."

John wiped his mouth with the linen napkin. He raised his right eyebrow and said, "I accept that. Welcome home, brother, and I'll do whatever I can to help ye and your business."

"Thank ye, I appreciate it. I know some folks, like Percy, won't be pleased with my returning. But Percy and I never did get along."

Kyle laughed. "Does a cow have spots? You two have fought since ye were in diapers."

"He started it."

Mother chimed in with her own riotous laughter. "The Lord be praised, I haven't heard that in years."

"Glad the boy can tickle ye, Mother." His father turned back toward Olin. "Bobby—"

"Olin, if ye don't mind, sir. I've not gone by Bobby since I left town."

"Olin it is, then. Why don't we start unpacking that wagon of yours?"

Olin pushed his chair back. "I have my things for tonight, 'tis all."

"Bobby?" His mother's voice quivered.

"Mother, I mean no disrespect, but it's good for me to establish my business, living at the shop. I promise I'll come home as often as possible." He flashed the smile that got him out of trouble more times than he could count. "My cookin' don't compare to yours."

"I wish ye would stay. It's safer," she mumbled.

Olin walked behind his mother and put his hands on her shoulders. "I'll be fine, Mum. The good Lord's taught me a few things about my anger. I haven't been in a fight since."

She nodded, but he could feel the tension in her body.

"Have ye met your pretty landlord?" Kyle smiled.

"Aye."

John got up from the table and picked up his plate and silverware. "Do ye remember Minnie Jacobs?"

Olin nodded. That gal didn't know how to keep her mouth still, from what he could remember of her.

"She's Ida Mae's cousin and, from what I hear, bends Ida Mae's ear quite often."

John's message was perfectly clear. Ida Mae no doubt knew all about him. If not before she rented the shop to him, certainly by the end of this day. "Thank ye."

"Come on, son. The sun be settin' soon."

"Yes, sir. Thanks for such a wonderful dinner, Mother." Olin bent down and gave her a kiss on the cheek. "It's good to be home."

She placed her wrinkled hand on his. Another twinge stabbed his heart. When had his mother aged so? With a brief squeeze, he extracted himself and went outside with his father to discuss the comments about his homecoming that had come up at the dinner table. Olin prayed he hadn't made a mistake coming back home.

three

Ida Mae stretched, trying to wake up. She snuggled deeper under the covers. Work demanded her attention. She tossed off the covers, went to the washbasin, and scrubbed the sleepy sand from her eyes.

The clanging of the storefront doorbell her father made had her glance at the clock and groan. *Today's going to be a wonderful day,* she mumbled, leaving her living area and running toward the front of the shop.

Peeking through the heavy linen curtain, she saw Olin Orr smiling without a care in the world. How could he be a murder? Shouldn't murderers look. . .evil? Speaking through the closed door, she asked, "What can I do for you, Mr. Orr?"

"I have your rent."

"I'm sorry." Looking down at her nightclothes, she asked, "Can you bring it back in half an hour?"

"As ye wish. May I bring my wagon to the barn?"

"Yes." Minnie's haunting words came back. Ida Mae fired off a quick prayer. "I'll be ready in thirty minutes."

He nodded, and his vibrant black hair bounced. Ida Mae suppressed the vain desire to run her fingers through his wavy locks. Her tactile senses were excellent for a spinner. Touch was so important in producing fine thread and yarn. But how does one resist such an urge for propriety's sake? She shook off her foolish ramblings and ran back to her room to dress. She didn't have time for entertaining such fanciful thoughts. Two hours behind and an order due this evening. Ida Mae would have to push herself hard.

The bell over the entrance jangled not more than thirty seconds after she'd unlocked the door and opened for business. Ida Mae turned, expecting to see Olin. Instead, John Alexander

Farres stood with his broad shoulders squared, wearing a trim, three-piece business suit. "Good morning, John Alexander."

"Morning, Ida Mae. I came to say I'll be pickin' up my order two days from now. I'm heading out of town on business and Mother said she could wait until my return."

"It will be ready."

John Alexander reached out and put his hand on her shoulder. "I know it will. Is it true that you married Cyrus yesterday?"

"No." Cyrus and Rosey had sworn her to secrecy. "How do you suppose that rumor started?"

John Alexander scratched his beard along his right jaw. "Half a dozen folks said they heard it from so-and-so, who supposedly heard it from Cyrus."

"I can't imagine who started the silly rumor, but I won't be marrying Cyrus."

A smile broadened on John Alexander's face. "Cyrus is a fine man, but I don't think he'd like having a wife who can handle financial matters as well as—if not better than—himself. I heard you rented out your father's blacksmith shop."

The delicate hairs on the back of her neck rose, sensing what? Fear? Concern that another would think her unable to discern good character in a person? "Yes."

"Heard he was a tin man from the north."

"From Pennsylvania."

"Not too fond of those Yankee traders. Took my uncle's winter cash one year, selling him a clock that didn't work and a bunch of tinware that fell apart the first time he poured something hot into the cup."

Did she dare tell him that he might be a local boy? "We shall have to see how good of a workman he is. He had high recommendations from those he worked with in Pennsylvania."

"I'll keep a watch out for you. I'll check on you when I come into town and see how you're faring."

"Thank you. It isn't necessary, but I appreciate your lookin' after me."

"Your pa wouldn't have it any other way."

John Alexander was ten years her senior. *He wouldn't make a bad husband*, she thought.

Sitting down at the spinning wheel, Ida Mae had just put her hand to the spindle when the bell over the door jangled again. This time it was Olin Orr. Not a glimpse of the smile she had seen thirty minutes prior remained. "Mr. Orr?"

"Here's your rent." He slapped the money down on the counter. "Do you have the papers for me to sign?"

Ida Mae got up, opened the locked cabinet door in her desk, and pulled out a rental agreement. "I've signed my name and dated it." She handed him the papers.

He read it over. "May I?"

He held his hand out for a pen. Ida Mae dipped the pen in the inkwell and handed it to him. He signed with a flare she hadn't seen in most men's handwriting.

"Thank you, Mr. Orr."

He nodded and left without saying another word. *What has him in knots?* she wondered.

"Most peculiar." Ida Mae went back to work.

She took a break at lunchtime and went to the lawyer's office to have the lease agreement for Cyrus drawn up. She wondered whether she should go back on her word and contact her brothers for their advice, but she'd already told Cyrus he could rent the property. In the end, she felt she'd spoken before prayer and proper consideration were given. Perhaps one day she'd learn to think before she spoke. On the other hand, it was only for one year and she didn't have time to seek out another tenant who would farm the land. She returned to the shop, picking up where she left off. Later that evening, Cyrus came in and she repeated the process of signing a lease with yet another tenant.

૨◆

Olin had been tempted not to sign the lease after seeing the man leave Ida Mae's shop moments before. It seemed strange the doors would still be locked at ten thirty, but seeing a man leave. . . Well, he'd seen those kinds of establishments up north. What bothered him most was that Ida Mae didn't seem to be that kind of a woman. And with her family farm, her spinster business, and now renting him the barn—how much money did she need?

Burning off steam, he worked through lunch. At two in the afternoon he finally sat down to eat, after retrieving a cool glass of water from the town water pump, twenty feet outside his business door.

"Bobby, is that you?"

Olin turned to a female voice he couldn't quite place.

"It is you. I heard the grapevine humming all day and just came to see for myself."

Olin smiled and opened his arms to embrace her. "It's good to see ye, Jane."

Jane gave him a hearty pat on the back. "I didn't believe it, but it is you. Heard you've gone Yankee on us."

A strangled chuckle escaped. "No, I just worked for them for a while. I learned a trade and thought I'd come home and put it to good use. Mother and Father wrote about how the tin men from the north were overpricing and selling less than good wares to area farmers, so I thought it would be good to have a local come work in the area."

She placed her hands on her hips. "Well, I'll be, you're so grown up. You became a man, huh?"

"I'd like to think so." Olin held back the memories of him and Jane and growing up together. Theirs had been a school-days romance. She had broken off their relationship, calling him immature. He reached for the nail barrel he'd been carrying from his wagon into the barn.

"Did you ever find your pot of gold?"

"In the Lord, yes. But no, I've given up on finding my fortunes in the gold mines."

She nodded and gave him an assessing glance from head to toe. "I believe you. Now, what's this I hear about you being a murderer? What really happened seven years ago?"

Olin set the small barrel down on the broad floorboards and offered it to Jane to sit on. He briefly went over the fight at the mine and the decisions that followed.

"I'd say you've got some enemies out there. Folks have been talkin' up a blue streak about it since you rolled into town. My husband—do you remember Richard Johansen from over the hill?"

Olin shook his head no.

"Oh. Never mind. Richard says the sheriff will be wantin' to talk with you, just because everyone is talkin' about it."

"I suspect he's right. So, you're married? Any children?"

"Four."

Olin raised his eyebrows and whistled. She didn't look like she'd even had one child. She'd always been a slender woman. "Four," he repeated in awe.

Jane rattled on for ten minutes about her family and life in Charlotte. She also mentioned that his landlord had apparently married last night, which explained the man leaving her office earlier this morning.

After Jane left, Olin worked his frustration out by scrubbing and cleaning the barn. Hard physical labor had always helped to release some of his pent-up frustrations. He knew the Lord was allowing this test for many reasons, but the primary one was to test his resolve to handle his anger. He knew now that coming home meant dealing with some of the issues he'd abandoned by running off to Pennsylvania seven years ago.

Thankfully he had worked up quite a sweat by the time the local sheriff came knocking.

"John Thatcher," the sheriff said, introducing himself and extending his hand.

The man stood like a thick chestnut tree: rugged, sturdy, and full of authority. Olin took the proffered hand and gave it a firm shake. "Heard ye might be coming around."

He lifted the brim of his hat off his forehead. "Word travels fast. What do you have to say about the past?"

" 'Tis in the past. I was found not at fault, but I still blame myself. I'm not the same man I was seven years ago. I don't know how to explain it apart from saying having a man die by my hand isn't something I enjoy living with."

"What makes you think your temper won't get the best of ya now?"

"I haven't lifted my hands to fight in seven years."

Sheriff Thatcher gave a slow nod. "Do ya mind if I come callin' from time to time?"

"No, sir. I reckon that's all part of your job."

"Good to meet you, Mr. Orr." He stepped back toward the doorway. "Are you any good?" He pointed to the tinsmithing equipment.

"My master taught me well and he was pleased."

"Good. We need an honest tradesman in the area. Are you still looking for gold?"

Olin let out a nervous chuckle. "No, sir. I gave that up, too."

The sheriff gave a final nod and slipped out.

Later, as Olin prepared for bed, he prayed. *Father, thank You for the grace and the strength to deal with my past. I know I'm a lowly sinner and that You've forgiven me, but I don't feel worthy. Bringing up all this past history today simply confirms how unworthy I am of Your grace. Forgive me again, Lord, for doubting Your will to have me return home.*

The loud crash of glass shattering, followed by a scream, jolted him out of his prayer.

❧

Ida Mae's heart raced. Fear sliced through her as a rock flew through the glass window in the east wall of her room. She pulled the quilt from the bed and wrapped it around herself for extra protection. Pressed against the room's southeast corner, the window on her right and the door to her left, she hoped to remain out of the way if another rock should fly through the now broken window.

Moments ticked by, silent except for the thunder of her heartbeat. Finally, she slid down, sat on the floor, and cried.

Sometimes life overwhelmed her. The lonely days since her parents' tragic deaths flooded her mind. Grief over the loss washed over her with an intensity she hadn't felt in months.

At some point she heard some rattling at the storefront's door. It was locked, but the door and the rest of the shop's west wall had windows. She huddled in closer to herself and stayed sequestered in the corner, hiding in the quilt. Shock had overtaken her senses.

"Miss McAuley, are ye all right?"

Ida Mae focused on the deer-like eyes. She closed her eyelids and opened them again and refocused. *Who?* She pulled the quilt closer.

"Shh, you're safe with me. What happened?"

Ida Mae just shook her head from side to side. Mr. Orr stood there holding a lantern over her.

"Let me help you up." He placed the lantern on the small table by the bed and lifted her as if she were nothing more than a feather. How heavy could tin be? He didn't appear to have huge muscles. He placed her on a chair and looked around the room.

"There's glass everywhere. Where's your broom?"

She pointed to the large closet that had been her parents' bedroom when they occasionally stayed in town.

He took two strides and crossed the room with ease. Admittedly her one-room living area was small—containing her bed and night table, chest of drawers, a couple chairs, and a small kitchen table near the cooking alcove—but to see him walk the width of the room in two steps. . . She wondered how long his legs were.

He went straight to work. Ida Mae sat there, numb, and watched. He was a handsome man, long legs and all. The heat of a flush brushed her cheeks. Ida Mae quelled her thoughts.

"What happened?" he repeated.

It finally dawned on her. "How'd you get in here?"

"I picked your lock. I heard the glass break so I was concerned that ye were injured, especially when ye didn't answer my knocking on your door. Who would throw a rock through your window? Where is your husband?"

"My husband?"

"Aye, shouldn't a newly married man be at his wife's side?"

"I'm not married." Then she remembered John Alexander and the news he'd heard. "It's a silly rumor with no bearing in fact."

"Oh, I assumed. . ." His words trailed off as he pushed the bits of broken glass into the dustpan.

Feeling more herself, Ida Mae jumped up from the chair. "Just what did you assume, Mr. Orr?"

"Forgive me. I assumed the man who left your establishment this morning was your husband."

"Man? What man?" Ida Mae replayed the day and realized what improper thoughts Mr. Orr had of her.

"Mr. Orr, you don't know me, so I'll forgive your rude insinuation. I am a woman of integrity. What you've entertained in your mind is simply unspeakable. The gentleman in question came in for business only." Ida Mae stammered. "Linen business. I am spinning for him."

"Forgive me." Olin Orr bowed. "It's been a rough day."

"Yes, it has, for both of us, I presume. Can I get you a cup of tea?"

"That would be wonderful, thank ye. I'll go to my shop and cut out a piece of wood to cover the broken window."

"Thank you."

"You're welcome. And please forgive my rude assumptions. If anyone should know better, it should be me."

Ida Mae stood there while he slipped out of the room and through the front door. The rumor that Olin Orr had killed a man was no longer rumor. The sheriff had come into the shop at closing and informed her it was the truth but that Olin had been found innocent, that it had been a death caused in defense of his own life. The sheriff's words had reassured her, but at the same time made her question Mr. Orr and his reasons for returning to a town where half of the people believed he'd killed a man in cold blood.

Ida Mae placed the half-full teapot on the stove. She covered her bed with the quilt, washed her hands and face, and placed a heavy housecoat over her nightclothes. Married? How was it that everyone thought she'd married Cyrus yesterday? She had a good mind to go back out to the farm and tell him in no uncertain terms to tell everyone that he'd married Rosey. On the other hand, he'd been telling folks for a long time that he asked Ida Mae to marry him, so it was human nature to assume that she'd been the one. But how could anyone know Cyrus had married? It didn't make any sense at all.

Ida Mae sighed. It had been a very long day and looked like it would be an even longer night.

She heard the banging of a hammer on the window frame and saw a large board over the broken window. It didn't take Mr. Orr long to fix the damage.

Olin knocked and Ida Mae opened the door to let him in, then quickly relocked it.

"All fixed. If ye purchase the glass I'll put it in for you," he said as he followed her to the table.

"Thank you." She poured the hot water into the china teapot to let the tea steep.

"Who do ye think would throw a rock through the window?" he asked as he sat down at the small table. The kitchen alcove contained a small stove that doubled for heating in the winter, a sink, and a few cabinets. It was large enough for the small table and a couple of chairs. Not that she entertained often.

"I don't know. Just some wild children, I imagine. There was no noise, no shouting. Just a rock crashing through."

She placed a teacup and saucer in front of him and another at her seat.

"I reckon you've heard the rumors about me."

Ida Mae nodded.

"If you're not comfortable with my renting from ye. . ."

She raised her hand. "No, I'm fine with you renting the shop. Sheriff Thatcher explained it all."

"I see."

She sat down. He looked down at his lap. "Mr. Orr, you should know that my parents died last year. Many of my parents' friends have taken it upon themselves to oversee my life. The sheriff is one such friend."

"I understand. I don't mean to pry into your business, but why are folks saying ye married yesterday?"

"The man who asked me to marry him, several times over the last year, got married yesterday and folks are just assuming it was to me. I promised him I wouldn't tell anyone who he married, but it's been a difficult day. I've had people coming and going all day, wanting to congratulate me, wondering why I was still working today and not enjoying my new married life."

Olin chuckled. "I'd forgotten how small this town really is. Living in the city of Philadelphia took awhile to adjust to, but there are some advantages to living in a place so large ye only know a handful of people. Down here, just about everyone is related."

Ida Mae had to agree.

Olin downed his tea. "I shall call it a night, Miss McAuley, and thank ye for the tea."

"Thank you for boarding up the window."

He stood up. "Ye probably need to sweep the floors again. I didn't find the rock."

Ida Mae nodded and Mr. Olin Orr retreated.

She picked up the broom and swept the floor. She reached first under the small chest of drawers, then the bed, using the broom handle. She knocked the rock out from under the bed. Wrapped around it was a piece of paper tied on by a piece of twine. Untying the note, she read, "Get rid of your tenant or else."

Earlier fear returned and slid down her spine like the shuttle on the loom.

four

Four days later, Olin still couldn't figure out why his landlord was avoiding him. Did it bother her that he'd come to her rescue? No doubt opening her locked door would give her an insecure feeling, but he had had little choice once he'd seen the broken window and heard the delicate cries. At least he felt that way at the time. Now he wasn't too sure. Mayhap he should have simply fixed the window and let her be.

Olin shook his head no. He knew better than that. He made his way down the road to his parents' house. He'd been invited to dinner, and his sister Janet and her family were going to be there, as well. Today had been different from the rest since his arrival. No one came to see if it really was him at the shop. Word must have gotten around enough so that people's curiosity had been settled.

He glanced at the peach trees laden with blossoms. After they ripened, the harvest would begin. He remembered the days he'd spent canning and preparing peaches with his mother. The entire family would get into the act. Among the gifts he'd brought for his mother had been two cases of canning jars and a new canning pot. He hoped a few of those filled jars would end up in his cabinet.

"Evenin', son." His father waved as Olin approached the main house. "How are ye doing?"

"Fine. The shop is all set up and I've even begun working on some pieces."

"Aye, 'tis good to keep a man busy."

"Aye. That it is, Pop. Looks like a good crop of peaches this year."

"Ye can thank your brother John for that. He's been pruning and keepin' those trees healthy for the past couple years."

John was a natural farmer and the oldest son. The farm would be his one day, as it should be. Kyle also had the ability and interest in farming, unlike Olin.

"Sheriff came by."

"My place, too."

"Seems like a good man."

"Aye. He actually talked with the owners of the mine before talking with me." Olin dismounted and tied the horse to the hitching post out front.

"Good. Percy hasn't been around."

"Good."

His father's bushy gray eyebrows rose on his forehead. "I imagine so. But the Good Book says to keep an eye on your enemies."

"Has Percy been in trouble since I left?" Olin hadn't been able to shake the feeling that Percy may have been responsible for the rock going through Ida Mae's window. After all, he did ask Kyle if he wanted to help run him out of town. *But why would he attack Ida Mae?*

"He's not a hard worker and hopes to get enough from his father's property so he doesn't have to work hard the rest of his life."

"If he doesn't work the land he won't get much from the property."

Kyle rounded the front porch, taking off a pair of work gloves. "Welcome home, little brother. How's the shop coming?"

"All set up, just waiting on orders to come in."

"Ye might be waiting for a spell. Percy's been telling folks you're just like those Yankee tin men."

"I suspected as much." He and Percy had always been like oil and water.

"Mother, on the other hand, has been bragging up a storm." Kyle rested his right foot on the second step.

Olin chuckled. "Mother would."

"It helps that you've sent her some of those tin cups and

pans over the years. She can claim just how good your work is.

"Pop, there's a problem with the grain chute in the barn for feeding the hogs. I tried working on it but I think the pin is shot. I'll need to run to town and order a piece." Kyle turned toward Olin. "Ye know, it would be nice if ye knew how to work Mr. McAuley's blacksmithing tools. We really need a new blacksmith."

"I'm not that skilled in blacksmithing, but I know how to do some small things. What do you need?"

Kyle pulled the worn pin from his hip pocket. "This here pin should be this thick the entire shaft. See how thin it is here and how it's bent?"

"Yup."

"Well. . ." Kyle went on to explain how the pin worked.

"Can I see where it fits the chute?"

"Sure." Kyle, Olin, and their father went off to the barn.

Olin examined the mechanism. "If I made a couple adjustments here"—Olin pointed to the pin—"and opened it here to receive a cotter pin, it might put less strain on the shaft."

His father scratched his chin. "Make both, son. That way if your idea doesn't work we'll still have a working pin."

"Fair enough."

"I see what you're suggesting, Bobby. I think it might work." Kyle leaned away from the chute.

"Ye boys go on discussing this. I best get back to your mother if I want some supper tonight. She sent me out to fetch a bucket of water fifteen minutes ago."

Kyle and Olin glanced at one another and grinned. Olin resigned himself to the fact that to his family, he would always be Bobby.

After Father left the barn, Kyle leaned back. "Percy really is set to run ye out of town. What did ye do to the man?"

"Nothing."

"Come on, this is me you're talkin' to. What happened between the two of ye seven years ago?"

"Nothing to say, apart from me trying to defend him."

"What? Ye mean after all this time you're saying Percy is the reason ye were fighting with Gary Jones?"

Olin shrugged. He shouldn't have said that much after all this time. What did it really matter anyway?

"Little brother, ye better watch your back. I'm afraid Percy isn't going to stop."

Like Father, Olin knew Percy didn't have the ambition to continue bullying him. One day Percy would tire of his attempt to get him kicked out of town. Olin hoped. "I imagine he'll tire of this."

They left the barn upon hearing a wagon pulling up. Janet's rich, black curly hair, so like his own, glistened in the sunlight. Four children jumped out as her husband secured the wagon. Olin smiled. Janet rushed over and gave him the best hug of his life. "Hey, little brother, it's good to see ye."

He squeezed her slightly and whispered in her ear. "It's good to be home."

"It's about time. Come meet my husband and our children."

❧

Ida Mae finished the jobs lined up for the rest of the week a day early. Today she planned to spend some time cleaning her living area and baking for tomorrow's church picnic.

Olin had replaced the glass in the window, but she'd been avoiding him. He made her feel things a single woman shouldn't. He lived too close; and to build up a friendship would take time and lots of space. She didn't dare share these thoughts with anyone, especially Olin.

Cyrus had come by a couple days ago and apologized again for the misunderstanding about his hopes and plans to rent the farm. And told her he was just as concerned as her about the rumors spreading around town regarding their marriage. He hinted that Rosey's parents would have their marriage dissolved if they found out about it. For the moment, she snuck out on occasion to join her husband on the farm. Ida Mae didn't think this was a wise way to start a marriage.

He had also mentioned he was turning the back forty acres

to help the soil for next year's planting. A part of her wanted to check on Cyrus's progress on the farm, yet another part of her didn't want to bother. Perhaps she should consider selling the land and purchasing a smaller cottage closer to town, as her brothers had suggested.

Minnie ran into the shop. "Ida Mae, you won't believe what I just heard."

"What's that?" Ida Mae looked over the next day's schedule.

"That Bobby Orr's cousin is trying to get him kicked out of town."

"What?"

"Percy says that Bobby has a horrible temper. He doesn't trust him and he's quite concerned about you. Percy says he has a mind to keep an eye on you just to make certain you're safe."

"You can tell Percy I'm just fine." Ida Mae slipped her hand into her pocket and fingered the crumpled note that had been tied to the rock. She'd read it a hundred times and prayed over it at least a thousand more. She didn't know if it referred to Cyrus Morgan or Olin Orr. In either event, she wouldn't give in to such tactics. After all, she had roots from the Hornet's Nest, as the British had referred to this part of the country during the Revolution.

"Why aren't you working today?"

"Finished all the jobs. I thought I'd give my room a good cleaning and prepare some food for tomorrow's church picnic." Ida Mae led Minnie to her private living area.

"Wonderful. Mother's packed a bunch of pickles and spring vegetables for the picnic. Father's donating a couple chickens."

Ida Mae had already heard someone was donating an entire hog. She imagined they had started to cook the pig in the pit. It would take close to twenty-four hours to roast. They walked into the small kitchen area, Minnie sat down, and Ida Mae went to the cupboard. "I think I'll make some biscuits."

"You do make a fluffy biscuit," Minnie said. "Why do you think Percy is trying to get Bobby to leave town? The way I heard it, the fight was self-defense."

How the gossips will change their thinking, she mused. "I don't know. I don't know Mr. Orr all that well. I think I've only seen him maybe thirty minutes since he moved in."

"As good a-lookin' as he is? Why, he could visit me as often as he'd like. Have you ever seen such unruly curls on a man?"

Ida Mae turned away from her cousin. "Can't say that I have."

"By the way, I heard someone broke one of your windows." Minnie put her feet up on the small footstool.

Four days. Minnie is slowing down. "Yes, I believe it might have been some boys."

"Who fixed it?"

Ida Mae grinned. She knew Minnie was fishing. "Mr. Orr. He heard the crash and came and lent me a hand."

"Guess it ain't all bad havin' a man livin' next door."

"No, it's not."

Minnie scanned the room. "Where's your ma's cranberry glass vase?"

Ida Mae turned and looked at the shelf where the vase usually sat. "I don't know."

❧

Olin came home in the dark. A single light burned in Ida Mae's room. He wondered about her and what her life must be like. He imagined it to be similar to his when he had lived in Pennsylvania with no family around. On the other hand, she did speak of her parents' friends keeping an eye out for her. And then there were her cousins in the area. She wasn't totally alone.

A shadowy figure slipped past the rear of her building.

"Whoa, boy."

His horse snorted.

Olin waited a moment, then proceeded to where the shadow had disappeared. A bright light burned in the window across the alley. If anyone had walked by, he or she would cast a shadow across Ida Mae's building. Olin waited a moment longer. After the rock incident, he wasn't going to take any chances.

A moment later, the back door to Ida Mae's opened halfway. "Hello?" Ida Mae called out.

"It's just me, Miss McAuley—Olin Orr."

"Mr. Orr?"

"Yes, I'm returning home from dinner with my family. Is everything all right?"

"Ah." She paused. "If it is only you, I guess so."

"Miss McAuley, has something happened?"

"No, I suppose not. It just felt like someone was—oh, never mind. I'm just being foolish."

Olin nudged his horse closer to the back doorway of Ida Mae's private quarters. "Are you certain you're safe? What happened?"

"Nothing. I guess it just seemed like someone was hovering around my back door."

"Give me your lantern." He hopped off his horse.

When she returned with a lantern, he reached out for it. Their fingers touched. Hers were warm, soft. His stomach did a flip. "Step back inside. I'll check the ground for any noticeable tracks."

"Thank you."

Olin searched the ground carefully. It was difficult to see, but everything appeared to be in order. None of the various-sized tracks seemed to indicate that anyone had been loitering there. He knocked on the door. "Miss McAuley, no one is around; you're safe."

She opened the door. "Thank you. I'm just being fearful."

"You have reason to be."

"Why? What are you not telling me?"

"I didn't mean to alarm you, Miss. I was referrin' to what my parents told me about the loss of your parents in the fire. Anyone in your circumstance would feel a wee bit alone and scared."

"Oh."

"Forgive me, but if ye are fearful of me renting from you, I'll find a new location."

"No, this has nothing to do with you."

"Very well." He bowed slightly and walked over to his horse. "I'll see you on the morrow."

They said their good-byes and he walked his horse around to the livery stable on the side of his portion of the building. After the animal was unpacked and ready for the night, Olin worked his way into his small room, a tool and storage area in the workshop he had converted to basic living quarters. It didn't compare to the lovely living area that Ida Mae had made for herself, but it was functional and served his purposes.

A gentle knock echoed through the room. "Hello!" he called out.

"Mr. Orr, may I come in?" Her voice sounded close yet muffled.

"Yes." He waited to see where Ida Mae was coming from. A noise came from the closet so he opened the door. A panel serving as a hidden door opened in the wall that joined their two parts of the building. There was no handle on his side.

"Please come in," he said, stepping back.

Ida Mae stepped through the closet and into the room. "I hope I didn't alarm you, Mr. Orr. My father built this passage-way for my mother so she wouldn't have to go out around the building to speak with him. Given what happened. . ." Her voice trailed off.

"How can I help ye, Miss McAuley?"

"I've been less than honest with you, Mr. Orr." Ida Mae stepped up beside him. She pulled a wrinkled piece of paper from her pocket.

He took the worn paper and read, "Get rid of your tenant or else." "I'll leave in the morning. I'll stay with my parents until I find a new location for my shop."

"No. I don't like giving in to idle threats."

"Ye know my history. I can't put you at risk."

"Minnie says your cousin Percy is. . ."

"Trying to have me kicked out of town." He finished her sentence. "Aye, I know. Ye don't need this kind of trouble in your life. I'll leave immediately."

"I appreciate your concern for my well-being, but I'm not certain this note pertains to you. I rented my parents' farmhouse to Cyrus Morgan."

"The man everyone claims you married?"

"Yes." She let out a nervous giggle that played havoc with his senses. "He might be the person someone is trying to get rid of."

"For what possible reason?"

The knit of her eyebrows told him there was nothing in Cyrus Morgan's past that would cause such a warning. "Ida Mae, ye must realize"—he brushed his hair from his eyes—"they're after me. Perhaps it was wrong for me to return."

She looked pointedly at the curls brushing his shoulders. "You need a haircut?"

"I've been meaning to have it cut."

"Would you like me to?" she offered shyly. "My mother taught me how to cut my older brothers' hair."

"Aye," he whispered.

five

Ida Mae savored every stroke of her fingers through Olin's hair. "Finished."

Olin opened his brown eyes wide. Wild energy targeted her. He hooded his eyes once again and reopened them slowly. The warm glow of a lightly creamed coffee came to mind.

Ida Mae swallowed, grateful they had cut his hair in the barn with the door wide open for anyone to see they were not acting improperly.

"Thank ye." He cleared his throat. "I'll move my personal items out tomorrow after church."

"Please don't." She bit her lower lip, not wanting to say another word.

"Ida Mae, ye must be protected. I don't know who sent this note, but I daresay it could be my cousin, or it could be someone else, someone more violent. It is not wise for me to live here and put ye in harm's way. Besides, my mum will be thrilled to have me living at home."

Ida Mae smiled. Parents could be like that.

"Thank ye for the haircut. I'll see ye in the morning. But before I go to bed I'll take one last look around the place. Don't forget to lock your doors."

She acknowledged his warning, slipped back into her own section of the building, and did as he instructed.

❧

The next morning, Ida Mae readied for church and the picnic. Walking the length of the town to the church, she left her biscuits in the fellowship hall where the women would prepare for the dinner outside. The church seemed full this morning. Many came in anticipation of the meal, as usual. The message given by the preacher reminded her of the need to walk in faith.

"Good morning, Miss McAuley." Olin Orr came up beside her at the park and smiled.

Earlier she had tried to scan the congregation for him but couldn't see him through the sea of people. "Good morning, Mr. Orr."

"Bobby!" A woman a handful of years older than Ida Mae waved.

"There's my sister, Janet. She's been anxious to speak with me all week. Would ye care to join us?"

"Thank you, but. . ."

He reached out his hand. "My mum can't wait to thank ye for the haircut."

Ida Mae let her hand rest in his. It was a strong hand.

After several introductions Ida Mae settled on a blanket next to Olin's oldest brother, John. "Fine day," he said.

"Yes, it is. Perfect for a picnic."

"Aye. Are ye plannin' on enterin' any of the competitions?"

"No, I'm fond of just being a spectator."

Cyrus Morgan strolled by with his hands in his pockets. "Afternoon, Ida Mae. How are you?"

"Fine."

She could feel John's watchful gaze. She'd love to ask Cyrus how Rosey was, but that would clue in the entire town that Rosey and Cyrus had married. "How's the farm?"

"Good. I'm planting corn this week."

" 'Tis a bit late in the season to be plantin' corn," John offered as he reached for a fresh strawberry.

"I'm praying for a late winter."

"Cyrus just rented the farm from me. He hasn't had the normal time to plant as he just finished rebuilding the house." Ida Mae defended him but checked herself from going further. Cyrus could have planted the corn earlier, before completing the house, if he had bothered to speak to her about his plans.

Cyrus's glance flickered between her and John. John reached over and rested his hand on the blanket behind her, as if letting Cyrus know that the Orr family had taken her under its wings. Without a doubt, Olin must have shared with his brother the threatening note.

As Cyrus made his farewells, she turned to John and waited for Cyrus to leave them, and then spoke. "That wasn't necessary."

"Unfortunately, I believe it may be. Bobby told Kyle and me what's been going on at your home. And I've personally heard the rumor Cyrus has been spreading, claiming he married you."

"You heard him say that?"

"Not in so many words, but he strongly implied it. He's a lazy farmer. Ye should have asked Kyle or me to work your land. We would have brought ye in a profit."

Ida Mae smiled. "You probably would have. I was just so startled to hear his plans and meet his wife."

"So, he did marry?"

"Yes."

"Who?"

"He's asked to keep that private. He's hoping to tell her parents after the harvest."

"I don't like it."

"I'm not fond of it, either. But I wasn't doing anything with the land. He's certainly turning the soil over."

John snickered. "Ain't no use in doing that more than a time or two in the late winter, early spring."

"No, I suppose it isn't. But he's been good to me, and he rebuilt the house."

"Aye, I'll give the man that."

Olin returned with two cups of iced tea. "Would ye like one, John?"

"Nope. It's my turn to enter the sack race."

John left and Olin took his brother's place on the blanket beside her. "You told your family?" she whispered.

"Just John and Kyle. I wanted them to understand why I was moving back home. Mother and Father are just happy to have me back. But I wanted my brothers to know I wasn't after their inheritance."

"Do your brothers believe you about what happened years ago?"

"Aye, even though they know my anger. I have a good family."

"You are blessed."

"Uncle Bobby," one of the twins squealed, running up to him with open arms and strawberry juice running down her chin.

Ida Mae's heart clenched. She missed her brothers. She missed her family. It was like Olin said last night—she was alone, so very alone.

≈

Olin watched Ida Mae closely throughout the day. His family took turns speaking with her one at a time. She blended well with them. As the day wore on, she relaxed perceptibly. He couldn't have asked for a better opportunity than what the picnic had produced. Between him and his brothers they each took a stroll down to her shop and inspected the outside for any possible trouble. Ida Mae didn't know it, but they were going to be watching her closely over the next few days.

He finally met Cyrus Morgan. John had pointed him out during the picnic. A young woman with strawberry blond hair kept a watchful eye on Cyrus all day. Olin speculated she was Cyrus's secret wife.

By evening the picnic broke up. He escorted Ida Mae back to her shop. He took advantage of the fact that he, too, had to go that way to pack his wagon and move back home. "Wonderful day, wasn't it?"

"I had a great time. You have a nice family."

"Aye, but they can run all over you if you're not careful."

Ida Mae giggled. "Your nieces and nephews are precious."

"Aye, even if they do stain my best dress shirt with strawberry juice."

"I can get that out."

"Thank ye for offering, but Mum will be able to."

"I reckon that she's done it a time or two. She loves her grandchildren."

He smiled. "Mum loves all her children. She's always been full of love. I didn't appreciate it in my youth. I felt suffocated. There's no reason I should have had such a temper and an anger streak meaner than any mountain lion. I'm not sure where that came from. My father never showed any signs of a temper, and neither do my brothers. I used to wonder if I was an orphan left on their doorstep, until I noticed the strong family resemblance between me and my mum's father."

"You're a handsome man." A deep crimson blush covered Ida Mae's cheeks.

Olin's chest puffed out slightly. "I thank ye for sayin' so. You're a mighty fine lass yourself."

"Forgive me, we shouldn't. . . ."

Olin wrapped his arm around her shoulders, then quickly removed it.

Ida Mae looked down at her feet.

"I didn't mean that the way it sounded, Ida Mae. I just moved back to town. I don't own anything and. . ."

She lifted her head and gazed into his eyes. "You're right. I'm just getting my parents' estate settled now. My brothers and I are finally at a place where we can decide who gets what."

"Ye know, a man would be foolish not to marry a lass such as yourself. With all your land and properties, ye would make him rather well-off."

Ida Mae stopped.

Olin noticed she no longer followed and stopped a couple paces ahead of her. Her eyes widened and she lifted her right eyebrow.

"What, what's the matter?"

"Forgive me, I've got to go." She marched toward her building.

Olin watched and waited until she slipped safely through the doorway.

ঽ

Ida Mae tossed and turned all night. Olin's words swirled

around in her mind like the spool of thread on her spinning wheel. Why hadn't she thought of that before? If she were to marry, the law stated that the man would assume the rights to oversee all of her properties. New doubts about Cyrus surfaced, not to mention Olin and his family. John had made it perfectly clear that he and Kyle would inherit their father's farm, not Olin.

Could he have thrown the rock through the window? He was outside her back door at the time she thought she had heard something.

After hours of remembering her moments with Olin, she no longer felt that way. She was glad he was moving to his parents' house. Her heart would be safer now. *Dear Lord, give me strength.*

The next morning she spent hours searching the shop for her favorite shears.

"Good morning, Ida Mae. How are you today?"

"Fine, and yourself, Mrs. Connors?"

"God's been blessing my boy. The corn is sprouting and nearly a foot tall already. The cotton is coming in, as well."

John's words about Cyrus planting late in the season came back. "What can I help you with, Mrs. Connors?"

"I wondered if you could spin this." She lifted a cloth covering a basket full of fur. Ida Mae lifted a few strands of the soft hairs. It would take some work but she could probably do it. "I reckon I can."

Mrs. Connors' smile went from ear to ear. "Thank you. Will it cost much?"

"It will take some time. I'll try to give you a good price."

"Thank you. I want to knit a lap blanket with it, help remind my boy of his favorite rabbit."

Ida Mae wouldn't question the woman's reasons for asking her to spin rabbit fur. Income was income. "How soon do you need this?"

"Next week should give me plenty of time."

After the woman left, Ida Mae gave in to her senses and

chuckled all the way to the spinning wheel. The fur was soft and it would make a fine yarn, perhaps too fine. The question was: Would the fur bind with the other hairs to make a strong enough yarn for knitting? "Wouldn't it have been easier to tan the hide with the fur on?" she mused.

"Tan whose hide?" Olin asked as he closed the door.

What happened to her bell? Ida Mae looked up to where the bell once hung over the door. "I can't believe it."

"What?" Olin spun around, looking behind him.

"My bell is missing."

Olin looked up at the hook that once held the bell. "I'll fix ye up with another. Is anything else missing?"

"I couldn't find my shears this morning, and Minnie noticed my mother's cranberry glass vase missing the other day."

"Ida Mae, is there someplace safer where ye could live?"

"No, there's only here and the farm, and I don't want to live at the farm with Cyrus and. . ." She cut off her words before she broke confidence with Cyrus.

"My guess is Rosey Turner," Olin supplied.

"You didn't hear it from me."

"No, but I watched folks at the picnic, and she was the only one who couldn't keep her eyes off of Cyrus."

Ida Mae smiled. "Well, that's good for young love, right?"

"Right." He stepped farther into the shop. "With your indulgence, Ida Mae, I'll be workin' late this evening. Will that be a problem?"

"No. As I said before, you could have stayed here."

"I still think it best. I hope that whoever sent ye that note saw me pack my wagon and move back to my house. I've been asking around for a new place to rent. Unfortunately, several folks have come needing some help with basic blacksmithing. I don't know much about that skill, but I picked up a few things along the years. I can make a set of shoes fit the horse, and a few other simple things, like nails and such."

"A town always needs a good blacksmith. I'm glad you can help folks out."

"Ye should place an advertisement for a blacksmith. I really work better with tin."

Ida Mac clutched the counter to steady herself. How could she be taken in by the stranger's charms so quickly? Cutting his hair had unraveled her sensibilities.

❧

Olin wanted to stay the night and watch over Ida Mae's place. Instead, he had arranged for Kyle to keep watch in the shadows. The only way for Olin's plan to work would be if he truly went back to his parents' house tonight and tomorrow night. How long he would be followed, *if* he would be followed, he didn't know.

He bade Ida Mae good-bye and couldn't help noticing the tension that grew in her as he left her shop. *Father, protect her,* he prayed as he saddled his horse for home.

He returned home and, with a great deal of self-control, managed not to wear a hole in the parlor's braided rug.

Kyle came home close to midnight.

"Anything?"

"Not even a stray rat. Are ye sure there's a problem?" Kyle flopped down in the chair by the large window in the living room.

"The bell over her door went missing today. Now why would someone take that bell unless they were plannin' on sneakin' into the place?"

"Don't know, little brother, but ye got your hands full with this one. John will be out there tomorrow night, but you'll have to be there the night after that."

"I know." Olin walked over to his brother and placed a hand on his shoulder. "Thank ye for your help."

"Is there a wedding in the near future?"

Olin huffed. "She'd make a fine wife one day, I think."

Remembering her touch, his gut felt like a piece of tin under the hammer, being shaped into something new. The tender touch of her fingers reminded him of a gentle summer rain.

"I need to call it a night, little brother. Perhaps we could spend the night in your shop rather than come back so late."

"Not for a few days. If there is someone watching her, I don't want him to know that we're watching for him."

"I hope ye are wrong."

"I do, too."

After saying good night to his brother, Olin returned to his childhood bedroom. At one time he had shared this room with Kyle. He now had one of their sisters' rooms. Olin wondered when Kyle would find a wife and move on to his own section of the farm. John, as the oldest brother, would inherit the main house. But there was the old log cabin in the side acres of the property. Perhaps Kyle planned to move in there one day.

Olin stretched and slipped under the covers. Tonight he would trust the Lord to keep Ida Mae safe.

❧

A week later he found himself crawling into bed after still seeing no sign of someone watching Ida Mae's. Perhaps he'd been wrong to assume. And she hadn't said anything about any other objects being missing. He made a crude bell out of the iron her father had in his shop. Someday he hoped to find the original bell, or replace it with a shiny brass bell.

The next morning while Olin was at work, Ida Mae walked into the shop from the street entrance. "Olin?"

He looked up.

"We need to talk."

six

Ida Mae knit her fingers together to keep them from shaking.

"What can I do for ye?" Olin set aside what appeared to be a large pair of shears.

"I saw you last night."

"Pardon?"

Ida Mae squared her shoulders and grasped her hips. The familiar scent of a recent open coal fire filled her nostrils. Memories of her father and the hours she'd spent with him in here aroused a tingling sensation that traipsed down her spine. She fought the memory and recaptured her resolve to address this man. "I saw you hiding around the corner of the building behind mine last night. What's going on?"

He picked up a metal rod and rolled it in his stained fingers. His focus remained on his hands as seconds chipped away at her unyielding stare, then he captured her gaze with his deep brown eyes. "My brothers and I have been keepin' watch every night since I moved out, to be certain that ye were safe."

How could she tell him she was grateful but at the same time resented the overprotectiveness? Nothing had happened in days. Seven days, to be precise. The same amount of time since Olin no longer lived there. Which gave credence to the possibility that the note was about Olin and not Cyrus. "Olin, I appreciate the concern but. . ."

He closed the distance between them. "Ida Mae, I think all this trouble is because of me. The least I can do is watch over you."

"Won't they see you in the shadows like I did?"

Olin reached out toward her, then quickly pulled back his hand. Ida Mae didn't know whether to be pleased or disappointed. One thing was certain, since Olin Orr had

51

arrived, her life had not been the same. She couldn't even think straight.

"Aye, it is possible. I shall be more careful."

"No. I don't want you out there. Whoever is out there isn't causing any further problems. Stay home, Olin."

He cocked his head to the right and raised his left eyebrow.

"I'm fine." She shifted her weight to her right hip. "I have a gun for protection and I know how to use it."

"Ida Mae. . ." He inched forward.

She stepped back. He stopped his approach, tossing the small rod down on the bench where he'd been working. "As ye desire, miss." He took off his apron and hung it from a wooden peg. " 'Til the morrow, then."

Ida Mae clenched her jaw to keep from saying she wanted him to watch out for her. She wanted him to stay overnight in his shop. She felt safer knowing he was there. Instead, she gave in to Minnie's insistence that things would be better when Olin moved his shop.

The walls of the tiny room seemed to move in around her. Ida Mae scurried out of Olin's shop through the hidden doorway.

❧

Leaning farther into the shadows, he watched as Olin Orr left his shop. "Where is she?"

Olin left with his horse. He'd stopped following him the third night. The first night, he followed Olin back to his family farm. The second night he followed him to the edge of it; the third night to the edge of town, where he watched Olin go down the outbound road toward his house.

"Did he hurt her?" Sweat filled his palms. He rubbed them on his trousers. He eased his head out slowly for a better view. A quick glance told him no one would see him. With his hands in his pockets, he walked down the street as if he hadn't a care in the world.

He snatched a look at the lock on the blacksmith's shop door. If she was in there, she was locked in. He walked three more blocks, then one block south. The back of Ida Mae's building loomed in the distance. Ida Mae popped out the back door of her shop, on the side of the building.

He scratched his chin and waved as he walked past on the opposite side of the road. *She'll be mine soon.*

He smiled and tipped his hat.

❧

Olin raced back to the farm. John and Kyle were nowhere to be found. "Where are they?"

"Your brothers have an engagement at the Bowers'." His mother stepped into the parlor with a fresh vase of flowers.

"Oh."

Olin paced back and forth.

"What is it, dear?"

Olin stopped a couple feet from his mother. "Nothing really. I'm just concerned for Ida Mae. She's asked me not to keep watch over her."

His mother sat down in her sitting chair. "Aye, I can see her asking that."

"Why? Doesn't she know how dangerous it could be?"

"Perhaps ye aren't thinkin' with your head, son. Ye fancy the lass, yes?"

"Aye." Olin sat down in his father's chair. "But I can't entertain such foolish thoughts at this time in my life. I have nothing to offer a wife."

"The heart pays no never mind to such things. Yer father and I had nothin' when we married."

Olin nodded. He knew the stories.

"Bobby, if the good Lord wants ye to be together, He'll work it out. Seems to me, you're afraid to trust the Lord for Ida Mae's protection."

"It's not that." Olin paused. Did he trust the Lord?

"Son, ye always had a strong streak in ye to plow ahead and do what ye thought was best. Like deciding that because ye were the third son ye would have the smallest share of the land and moved on to make your way in this world without the help of your parents."

Olin took in a deep sigh.

"I say this not to remind ye of what happened but why it happened. In your father's will ye will inherit ten acres. It's been that way since the day ye were born. It's plenty of land for a man to provide for himself and a family if ye were to accept it. But ye told your father over and over again to give the land to Kyle. And while Kyle is planting those ten acres along with the other fifty he's to inherit, the land is not his. Ye could speak to your father and ask him for your inheritance if ye wish to marry one day."

Olin fought down the old argument that he didn't deserve the land after what he'd done to shame his family. Should he accept the gift? Should he pursue a relationship with Ida Mae?

"Have ye told Ida Mae how ye feel?"

"No. I don't know how I feel. I'm attracted to her, but she's always pulling away from me."

"Well, dear"—his mother slapped the arms of her chair and lifted herself out of it—"dinner is on the stove and your father shall return quickly. I don't see what all the fuss is about if ye haven't spoken your intentions."

"She's in danger, Mum."

"Aye, but what kind?"

His mother left him in the room to ponder her last comment. As Olin rolled it around, he had to wonder, was she really in danger or was it all about him? He had moved out and, with some luck, he'd find a new place to rent soon and would be permanently removed from Ida Mae's life. Whoever sent the warning wasn't out to hurt her, but rather to force him to leave the area. Perhaps if he showed Ida Mae a little interest the individual would let her be.

≈

Ida Mae stretched her back as she got up and walked around the shop. Sitting on the stool hour after hour had a certain disadvantage. She glanced up at the clock as the brass hammer struck three times. She twisted her body to the left, then the right, and caught a glimpse through the curtained window of the bright sunny day. With a roll of her shoulders, she decided to call it a day. Grabbing her bonnet from the peg by the door, she ventured out of the shop and walked down the street toward the center of town. A small fountain stood in the center of the marketplace. Ida Mae went over and sat on the outer wall with the fountain cascading behind her. People traveled quickly from place to place. Women held bundles and packages while the men loaded freight on their wagons. A lively melody streamed out of the pub. Everyone seemed to have a place to go, a place of belonging.

Chester Adams passed by with a brief wave and a smile.

Regan O'Malley swung a basket full of vegetables in perfect rhythm with her stride.

Then her eyes caught on Cyrus Morgan. She was too far away to hear the words exchanged between him and Mr. McGillis, the merchant of the Grain and Feed store, but Cyrus's rigid posture left little doubt that it was an unpleasant conversation. Cyrus boarded his wagon and slapped the reins. His horses—*correction, my father's horses*—whinnied and rushed the wagon down the street.

Mr. McGillis scanned the area. Seeing her, he marched over to the fountain. "Ida Mae!" He rubbed the dirt and sweat from his hands on a rag. "Cyrus Morgan says you're paying for all his orders. Is that true?"

"All?"

"Yes. I understand he's working on your farm, and there are expenses toward rebuilding the house, but a plow is an expensive item. I told him I had to check with you first. I'd say he didn't like that much."

I could see that. Ida Mae held back, then asked, "What kind of a plow does he say I need?"

"Another one like your father ordered a couple years back. It didn't make sense to me. He also ordered a bunch of hoes and rakes."

"Did he order any seed?"

"No, and that's the oddest part. If a man is going to be planting fields, he should have done it sooner, but he also needs to buy seed."

"Mr. McGillis, I appreciate your concern for my interest. I agree we don't need another plow. I'll speak to Cyrus about it. I would, however, like to order some seed. Corn and cotton is out of season for planting now. What do you recommend?"

"You could get some beans and other summer vegetables started now. Some winter squash might be good, as well."

"Thank you. I'll ride out to the farm this evening and look into Cyrus's plans."

"Very well. Thank you, Ida Mae."

"Thank you. Father would be so happy to see how his longtime friends continue to watch out for me."

"'Tis an honor, lass." With a tip of his hat, Mr. McGillis headed back to his shop.

Ida Mae nibbled her lower lip for a moment as she pondered this new information. She had to confront Cyrus Morgan and find out what was going on. John Orr had been right. Cyrus should have planted long ago. And what had happened to her father's plow?

She scurried back to her shop, changed into her riding dress, and grabbed her horse from the stable. The entire trip she prayed for wisdom. She wasn't surprised to find Cyrus sitting on the front porch with his feet up on the rail. Rosey brought him a tall glass of tea.

"Welcome, Ida Mae." Cyrus came to his feet. Rosey gave a slight smile. Cyrus beamed. "What brings you out here?"

"I just spoke with Mr. McGillis." Ida Mae decided to hit him hard and watch his reactions.

"Ah, I've been meaning to tell you about the plow."

"What about it?"

"I hit some bad patches of rock. Tore the plow right up. Without your father, there's no one else to fix it, so I was trying to order you a new plow."

Her father had worked this land for many years. There was no deep patch of rocks that she could recall. All that had been turned up years ago went to build the fireplaces, walkways, and root cellars. "Where'd ya hit rock?"

"Uh, over by the river."

"Why were you trying to plow over there?"

"Ida Mae, if you don't think my decisions are right, go and hire yourself another farmer." Cyrus stomped his foot.

Rosey's eyes widened but she didn't speak.

"Cyrus, I simply asked why."

"Ain't no need to explain to a woman. You ain't got no business sense at all."

"Cyrus, I happen to own this land, and you won't be speaking to me in such a manner."

Cyrus dropped his chin to his chest for a moment, then eased it up slowly. "You're right. I apologize. I don't fancy folks calling me a liar, and I'm still steamed at Mr. McGillis."

"Apology accepted. I can't afford a new plow this year. Perhaps when the harvest comes in. The expenses to rebuild were much higher than I anticipated. I've been going over the books and I'm just about ready to settle my parents' estate with my brothers."

"I'm sorry. I'll be more careful with the expenses. I built ya a fine house, though."

"Yes, you've done a wonderful job, thank you."

"Maybe I'm a better carpenter than a farmer."

Rosey coughed. "I think you did a mighty fine job on the house. I don't smell a bit of smoke in it except around the fireplaces where that would be natural."

"Thank ya, darlin'." Cyrus spun around after giving his wife a quick wink. "I'm sorry, Ida Mae. Is there anything I can do to make it up?"

Buy a new plow from your own money, she wanted to say, but she held her tongue. "No, I guess not. But I'll be renting the farm to someone else after the harvest."

"I could leave now." Cyrus's voice sounded strained.

"No, you and Rosey need a place. Do her parents know yet?"

"Not until the harvest."

Right. Cyrus's charms no longer worked. Ida Mae now knew he'd been taking advantage of her, and she was too smart a businesswoman to let him continue. She mounted her horse once again. "I'll be approving any order with Mr. McGillis before he fills it. Like I said, I have to be careful with my expenses for a while."

"I understand."

From her horse, she saw a small patch of summer vegetables growing. Cyrus couldn't have planted those. "Garden looks nice, Rosey."

"Thank you."

"She's a right fine catch." Cyrus wrapped his arm around his wife and pulled her closer to him.

Ida Mae's trip back to the town seemed longer than usual. Cyrus Morgan hadn't planted a thing. And what was he doing using the plow by the river? Something wasn't adding up. She'd be rid of him by fall. She prayed the Lord would have him understand it wasn't personal, just wise business.

Or was it?

seven

Unable to sleep, Olin tossed back his bedcovers and dressed. In the wee hours of the morning he rode back to town. A faint scent of smoke crossed his nostrils, intensifying as he got closer. He pushed the horse faster. Outside Ida Mae's private quarters a cast-iron barrel containing burning debris had fallen on the ground and rolled very close to the steps leading to the door. Olin hustled to the town well and pumped out a bucket of water. In a matter of minutes the fire was out.

Ida Mae opened the door a crack. "What's going on?"

"It's me, Olin, Ida Mae. I found this trash bucket on fire and was putting out the flames. Go back to bed. Everything is all right."

"Olin," she whispered, "I told you—"

"Shh," he said. "I'll speak with ye later."

She slammed the door. His back muscles tightened. Olin worked them until they relaxed. The fire appeared to be the result of someone carelessly knocking over the incinerator, rekindling the flames.

Olin search the ground for any sign of an animal, or a human animal, knocking over the barrel. Seeing no evidence, he breathed a sigh of temporary relief. He walked over to Ida Mae's door and tapped it twice. "Ida Mae, it is me."

"Olin, I told you—" She opened the door. He stepped across the threshold but stood in the doorway.

"I couldn't sleep so I rode into town to check on you."

"Olin, you have to stop. I'm fine."

"Are ye, lass?"

"Y–yes," she stammered.

He reached over and held her by the elbows. "Ida Mae, I am concerned for you."

"Olin, how can I trust you? Every time something happens, you're there, lurking in the shadows. Minnie says. . ." Her lips went silent.

Olin dropped his hands to his side. "Ye don't trust me?" He took a tentative step back.

"Olin," she whispered, "I don't know what to think."

He saw tears filling her eyes. "Ida Mae, I care about you. I would never hurt ye."

"I know, but Minnie—"

"Is a gossip," he finished for her. "I'm sorry, but she's been that way ever since she was a wee one."

"True."

"Minnie doesn't know who to believe or trust. Have I ever done anything to ye? Have I ever snuck into your home without an invitation? Well, except for the time when I picked the lock because of the broken window."

Ida Mae sniffled.

"My sweet bonnie lass. . ." He reached out and wiped the tear from her cheeks. "The good Lord as my witness, I would never hurt ye."

"I want to believe you." She sneezed into her handkerchief.

"Pray, and trust the Lord. I think the fire was an accident. Have ye had any other problems?"

"No. Well, yes, some." She explained what happened with Cyrus as they stepped outside and sat down on the back steps. She also mentioned the loss of a few other small items.

"No further threats?"

"No." She wrung her hands in her lap.

"What are ye not telling me, Ida Mae?"

"Minnie says you may have taken liberties with the sister of the man you killed."

The heat of anger pumped through his veins. He silently counted to ten and fired off a quick prayer. "Ida Mae, Gary Jones didn't have a sister."

"Ah, so it's another misspoken piece of information."

"Aye, I'm afraid so. I swear, Ida Mae, I've never been less

than a gentleman when in the presence of a woman."

She paused for a moment. "I believe you."

"Thank ye."

"Olin, I misplaced my mother's silver hairbrush earlier this week. Minnie said you probably took it to melt it down to cover a piece of tin."

"Of course I didn't, but ye are free to check my shop and my home if ye so desire."

"I don't believe it. I mean I'm trying not to believe all the things said about you. But sometimes it is just so hard."

"What have others said, if ye don't mind me askin'?"

"One of my customers has heard the same rumors Minnie has reported to me. Another suggested that John Thatcher doesn't trust you, that's why he's kept watch on your place."

"The sheriff?"

&

"Yes." Ida Mae held her sides. It was so easy to talk with Olin, and in his presence she believed him. How could she not be strong when Minnie reported all sorts of untruths to her? And why would Minnie care?

"I wasn't aware of his watching my shop. He's come in a time or two, but he came in regarding my work."

"What is the sheriff ordering?"

"Ah, lass, I'm afraid I can't tell ye. It's a confidential matter."

"Confidential tinsmith?"

Olin chuckled. "I was as shocked at the time the sheriff spoke with me, as anyone would be. But it is confidential."

Calm continued to sweep over her as she sat next to him. Inhaling deeply, her nostrils filled with the scent she'd come to know as Olin's. The hint of wood smoke, not coal, reminded her as to why they were here sitting on the back steps outside her room instead of inside. "Are you sure the fire was an accident?"

"Appears to be. But, Ida Mae, my concerns are increasing. Ye need to be safe. Why don't ye come stay at my parents' until we know who's behind all this."

"No." Ida Mae closed her eyes. Fire had caused her parents' deaths. Fear wove around her heart like a coarse thread. "Not yet. If you think the fire was an accident, then there isn't anything more to be concerned about."

"Aye, there is. Ye mentioned your mother's hairbrush. It appears to me someone is watching you, sneaking into your home, and stealing personal items. What if ye walk into your private quarters and startle the thief?"

"Olin, I've given this a lot of thought. It seems to be the actions of a child."

"Mayhap, but I believe caution is in order."

"Olin, I can't live in fear. It's taken me the better part of the year since my parents' deaths to even venture out in public settings. For the first few months after they died, depression ruled my days, then it switched to fear that I would die a horrible death, as well. Cyrus started rebuilding my parents' house right after the fire. He'd work evenings and weekends. You know that is what truly puzzles me about him. He worked in earnest to fix up the house, but his farming skills are—well, let's just say most ten-year-olds could do better."

Olin rested his arm around her shoulders.

"All of that is to say, I can't go back to living in fear. I have to face this, catch whoever it is in the act. If I go to your parents' house, I'll never find out who is doing all this."

"Have you told John Thatcher?"

"No. Well, I mentioned the bell missing from my shop door."

"Good, he needs to be aware."

She sensed Olin would be talking with the sheriff to apprise him of all the recent events.

"I should go back to bed."

"Aye." Olin stood up and brushed the backside of his pants. "I'll see ye in the morning."

"Sleep in your shop. Don't go home."

"Aye, it would be easier. And no one should be watching the shops now."

"Good night, Olin." She stood up and made her way to the top step, then turned back to look at him. "You're a good man, Olin."

In the shadowy light she could see his face brighten. *A very good man.*

"By the good Lord's grace; but ye are a fine lass." He opened the door for her, then slipped off into the darkness. Her heart plummeted. In spite of what Minnie had said, she felt safe with Olin. And her growing attraction deepened. It was no longer just his fine looks but him, his character, the way he treated her. Perhaps spending time at his parents' home would allow her to really get to know this mysterious man that trouble seemed to follow. *Perhaps.* She closed the door and secured it, grateful for the bolt lock her father put in so many years earlier.

૨ઢ

Olin woke to a thundering crash. He bolted up from his cot and tried to get his bearings. "Who's there?"

Seeing nothing, he slipped on his boots and worked his way to the front of the smithy. Opening the barn door allowed full light to flow into the area. Seeing nothing out of place, he ran around the corner of the building to Ida Mae's front door.

The iron handle wouldn't move. "Locked." He rattled the door in its hinges. "Ida Mae!"

The sign in the window said CLOSED. He didn't like it. He ran back to his shop and picked up the tools he needed to force entry. That's when he spotted the window. How had he missed it? Framed by shattered glass, Ida Mae stood looking out toward him. "Let me in, lass."

She stood for a moment looking past him, then shook her head slightly and walked toward the door.

He slipped through and had her in his arms before she'd fully opened the door. "Are ye all right?"

The blue in her eyes darkened. She said nothing. He held her closer and whispered in her ear. "You're safe now."

He swept her up into his arms and carried her over to the

area where the rock had been tossed. This rock was much larger than the one before. Carrying her to the back room, he gently set her on the chair. "I'll be right back."

She nodded, but not a word came from her lips.

He pulled himself away and went to the rock. A note was wrapped around this one, as well. He untied it and read the ugly message. A horrible word he couldn't even repeat blazed across the crumpled paper. Olin shoved it in his pocket and went back to Ida Mae.

He pulled out a carpetbag from her closet and shoved a dress, a couple of blouses, and a skirt into it. Then he went to her chest of drawers and pulled out some unmentionables, not bothering to ask if they were what she needed or not. "Come on. You're going to my parents' house. It isn't safe for you to be here alone and it isn't proper for me to stay to protect ye."

She seemed to be in shock. "Ida Mae?"

She closed her eyes, then opened them slowly. The deep blue of her eyes focused on him. "For a couple days, just until the window is fixed."

No way would he allow her to return until they caught who was behind all this.

They rode together on his horse. He wrapped his arms around her. Several people stared as they made their way out of town. He knew the tongues would be wagging after this, but what choice did he have? Whoever was after her had been there last night. He'd seen Olin come out of the building and assumed. . . Well, he wouldn't let his mind go to what the viper of a man had thought.

She didn't speak the entire trip to his parents' house. After a brief recap of the night's and morning's events, he left Ida Mae in his parents' able care. His father, Olin knew, would keep his rifle handy.

❧

Olin waited most of the day at the sheriff's office. Several townspeople had come in to report the broken window at Ida Mae's shop. Some of them looked at Olin as if he stank. But

Olin kept his mouth shut tight and answered questions only if they spoke to him. Fortunately, no one asked him anything more than if he was here to report the broken window. Which he was.

The door slammed open and Percy barged through. He stopped short upon seeing Olin. "Where is she?"

Olin stood up and squared his shoulders. "Safe."

"Why don't you go back north? You're not wanted here."

Olin sat back down.

"Minnie says it's all your fault. The broken window was meant for you."

Olin bit down harder. He knew the truth, and he wasn't about to give Percy any information that might go back to Minnie.

"What? Someone cut your tongue out?"

Olin narrowed his gaze and seared it into Percy as if it were red-hot metal ready to be molded and shaped.

"Ah, you were never anything but a yellow belly." Percy stomped out of the sheriff's office.

Olin closed his eyes and prayed for the Lord to remove his anger. He was certain his cousin had come once again to try to persuade the sheriff to run him out of town.

Finally, by mid-afternoon the sheriff strolled in. "Sheriff," Olin greeted with a nod as he stood.

"Mr. Orr, I heard we have a problem."

"Ye might say that."

"Folks say you hustled Ida Mae out of town, that she was screaming and hollering the entire time."

Olin snickered. "She didn't say a word. She's at my parents' farm. Safe."

John Thatcher removed his hat and nodded.

"Good, now tell me, what happened?"

Olin went over the entire history, starting with the first window and message. "Today, this was the message." Olin pulled the crumpled paper from his pocket and handed it over to the sheriff.

"I see. Have you had improper relations with Ida Mae?"

"No." Olin defended Ida Mae's honor perhaps a bit too loudly. "Don't ye see? The person who did this must have set the fire last night. They must've seen me leaving after having been inside for so long."

John Thatcher scratched the day-old growth on his chin. "This whole affair might cause Mr. Bechtler some concern about you making the mold for his gold coin mint."

"Aye, it wouldn't be much of a secret if the thief found the plates before I'm done with them."

"How long can Ida Mae stay at your folks' home?"

"As long as needed."

"That should work fine. You are aware the gossip will spread quickly that you've taken Ida Mae off. If she doesn't return to work tomorrow, they may start suspecting you."

"I'm aware. Please, go to my parents' farm and see that she's all right. She's in shock, but I expect her to be doing better now. Mum has a way with calming a person."

"That she does. I'll swing over to your farmstead and have a long talk with Ida Mae."

"Sheriff. . ." Olin looked down at his dusty boots. "She doesn't know about today's note."

"I'll be sensitive. But she's a grown woman and has a right to know."

"Aye. Who would say such horrible things about Ida Mae?"

A slow smile creased the leathered cheeks of John Thatcher. "You fancy her, don't you?"

"Aye. When all is settled I shall tell her of my feelings."

John slipped his hat back on his head. "I reckon she probably already knows."

eight

"Would you wash those spinach leaves, Ida Mae?"

"Yes, ma'am." Ida Mae went to the kitchen pump, pumped out a small amount of water, soaked the bright green leaves in the bucket, and shook out a handful. Preparing a meal for a small army hadn't been a part of her life for many years. She enjoyed it and she missed it.

"Bobby says ye be a fine spinster. How's your weavin'?"

"Fair. Mother was the best."

"Aye, that she was. Did ye know that my clansmen brought the flax to this country a hundred years ago?"

"No."

"Well, it be a fact, darlin'. Me maiden name is Steele. In 1718 Thomas Steele sailed from Ireland with a group of others to the New World, seekin' a place they could worship God and make an honest wage. The governor told them to head north. The French and Indian War was heating up at the time and the governor thought sending me clan out there would make a great first line of defense. What the governor didn't know was that the reverend was an old classmate with someone in the French army. I used to know who, but I don't keep these things straight."

Ida Mae watched the delightful woman work as she talked, quickly preparing the dough for the bread. Her own family lines came to America later but had moved away from the clans. She had many ancestors who were not Scots-Irish, unlike the Orr family.

"The Frenchman told his Indian friends to leave this group of people alone and they were never attacked during the war."

Ida Mae giggled. "I reckon the governor wasn't pleased."

"I always pictured him just standing there scratching his wig, trying to figure out what these Presbyterians did to keep the Indians away. The Puritans considered our people a rowdy sort. In the end, it was that ship of people who brought the potato and linen flax to the New World. Many say that without us the War of Independence would not have been fought."

"How do you know so much about your family?"

"Me mum and pa passed it down. There's another story about the Great Wagon Road, but we'll save it for another time."

Ida Mae wanted to hear it now. It had been so long since she'd been around a real family. Her stomach flipped. Memories resurfaced. Ida Mae dipped her hand back in the bucket and shook out some more of the leafy greens. The Orr farm was already producing peas, beans, spinach, and radishes. Cyrus hadn't even started to plant the seed yet. What had she gotten herself into letting him rent the farm and house?

"Ida Mae, I told ye that story about my family because we come from good stock. Ye can trust Bobby—Olin," she amended.

Bobby, she mused. He didn't seem like a Bobby to her. Olin fit him better.

Mrs. Orr went on and on about her family's history. While the facts were interesting, the information wasn't enough to keep Ida Mae's mind from drifting back to seeing that rock come through the front window. If she had taken one more step she would have been hurt, if not killed. Who was so angry with her for letting Olin rent her father's shop? It didn't make sense.

"Ida Mae?"

"Sorry, my mind drifted."

"That's all right, dear. I can rattle on a bit about family history. It goes back hundreds of years. . . ."

Hundreds. Ida Mae raised the corners of her lips and hoped the smile appeared genuine.

Mrs. Orr giggled. "I won't be putting ye through all that.

I'm just trying to distract ye from dwellin' on your shop. Which I be doin' rather poorly."

"I'm sorry. I don't understand why someone would be attacking me in such a way."

"Rumors. And mind ye, these are just rumors. Word was that someone deliberately attempted to start a fight with Bobby all those years ago. His father and I decided we needed to remove him from the area and arranged the apprenticeship. I reckon we figured enough time had passed and no one would hold a grudge for seven years. Mayhap we be wrong. I'm so sorry."

"But that's what is odd. Why haven't they attacked Olin's shop? Why mine? If someone were truly out to ruin Olin, wouldn't they send rocks through his windows?"

Mrs. Orr raised her right eyebrow.

"There aren't any glass windows in his shop, but still."

"Ye might be right. But why would anyone want to hurt a bonnie lass such as yourself?"

"I don't know. I wish I did, but nothing has made sense since Olin came to town."

"Then marry my boy and be done with it."

"Pardon?"

❧

"Afternoon, Sheriff, what can I do for you?" Olin put the hammer down and walked over to meet the sheriff.

"I had a visit from one of Ida Mae's neighbors. They say they saw you out last night behind Ida Mae's and setting the fire."

"What?"

Sheriff Thatcher held up his hands. "Hold on. That's what they said. I pushed them further and they admitted that they didn't see you start the fire. They just assumed that Ida Mae caught you and you put it out."

The vein on Olin's right temple started to pulse.

"Seems to me someone is anxious to get you out of town, or at least far away from Ida Mae."

Olin crossed his arms and leaned back on the beam holding the corner of the loft. "I feared that be the case. I'll move my business out today."

"Lawrence McGillis at the Grain and Feed store says he has a back room where you can set up shop. The only problem is it isn't within eyeshot to watch over Ida Mae's. My wife won't appreciate it, but I'll spend the next couple of nights here in the loft. I should be able to sneak in early enough so no one will know I'm inside."

"There's a secret passageway between her private quarters and my shop. I don't know how to get into her place from here, if there is a way, but on her side it's a door in the back of the closet."

"Show me."

Olin pointed out the opening and together they went around to the front and then inside Ida Mae's shop. Olin leaned over and pulled out two thin rods, one with a small hook on the end. He inserted them into the keyhole and jiggled them into place, then opened the door.

"How many folks know you can open a lock like that?"

"Ida Mae does. Apart from her, I don't think there's anyone else."

"Let's keep it that way, or you'll be blamed for every crime in the area."

"Yes, sir." Olin slipped his tools into his pocket. They went past the counter in her shop and entered Ida Mae's private quarters. The sheriff scanned the orderly room. He appeared quite at ease being in someone else's home when it was vacant. Olin felt as uncomfortable as a man sitting in church with wet clothes. It didn't seem right for him to be standing in the room without her. In the full light of day he saw that she'd taken the small area and made it quite warm and welcoming.

"Where's the secret doorway?"

"Over here." Olin pointed to the door in the back of the large storage closet against the wall of the smithy.

The sheriff examined both sides of the entryway. "While

I'm keeping watch I'll want this doorway open. But if I don't catch who's behind all this red-handed I'll want you to nail your closet door shut in these corners. If the thief has been using this passage to sneak out through the barn, maybe we can trap him in your closet."

"I don't want Ida Mae in any danger."

"Nor do I. The best thing to do is to keep things as normal as possible. What concerns me is the note on the rock this morning. By now the entire town knows you brought Ida Mae to your family farm. Let's keep it that way. Tomorrow, bring her back and I'll watch over her all night. Those two nights should give me a chance to catch this guy. If he is simply taking things out of her place, then he'll want to come in while Ida Mae isn't home and while the building is vacant. I'll be there ready and waiting. If, however, they are after her, they'll wait until tomorrow night when she appears to be vulnerable."

"I don't like it. What if something happens to her?"

"You'll have to trust me. Don't try takin' the law into your own hands again, son. You know what happened the last time."

Olin's stomach soured. "Fine."

"Olin." The sheriff placed his hand on Olin's shoulder. "Trust me."

"What if nothing happens in the next two days?"

"We'll decide what to do then, agreed?"

"Agreed."

They left Ida Mae's shop. Olin checked the boards he'd put up to cover the broken window. All was secure. Back in the smithy he packed up his tools, then went over to the Grain and Feed shop to speak with Mr. McGillis. They agreed on a fair price, and the rest of the day Olin spent moving and setting up his shop in the new location. He drew up a note telling folks where to find him. Anything to put Ida Mae in a safe position.

"So, you're leaving town?" Percy stood in the doorway with a smug grin.

❧

"Ida Mae, sit, please." Mrs. Orr rubbed her hands on the skirt of her apron.

Ida Mae sat down at the small kitchen table. "Mrs. Orr, Olin and I aren't—"

"Ye have eyes for one another. Anyone can see."

Ida Mae cast her eyes toward her apron.

"Darlin', ye and Bobby—Olin—snatch glances at one another all the time. If ye love him. . ."

"We haven't spoken of such matters."

"Ah, me boy is takin' his sweet time. I thought with him having his brothers out all night, watchin' over your place, that ye and he were closer."

"No, ma'am."

"Do ye love him?"

Ida Mae's fingers started to shake. She laced them around the hem of her apron. "I'm attracted to him, but love? It is too soon to tell."

"Aye, I understand. Ye love him, but ye don't know it yet. That's fine. What I was thinkin', and mayhap it be an old woman's need for more grandchildren, is ye and Olin could marry and perhaps this would stop the person."

"I can't marry Olin."

The screen door to the kitchen slapped shut.

"Mum, what are ye suggesting?"

Mrs. Orr's face turned a brilliant shade of crimson. "Foolish thoughts, an old woman's foolish thoughts. Forgive me, son. Forgive me, Ida Mae."

"Forgiven." Ida Mae grasped the hem of the apron so tightly her fingers started to numb.

Mrs. Orr scurried out of the kitchen. Olin sat down beside Ida Mae. "I'm sorry."

"Olin, she was just probing."

"Aye. I daresay something she is quite proficient at. I had a talk with Sheriff Thatcher. He's going to stay in my shop overnight and hope to catch whoever is slipping in and removing items from your shop and personal quarters." He went on to explain in greater detail about moving his business and the two-day plan to watch the place. He concluded with, "Percy came to see me as I was getting ready to close up the shop."

"Oh?"

"He heard I was leaving town."

Ida Mae shook her head. "The gossip in this town can be incredible."

"Yes, and today a couple of your neighbors came to the sheriff to report that I had attempted to start a fire last night."

A wave of doubt instantly rose and fell in her stomach.

"Ida Mae, the sheriff questioned them thoroughly and found they never saw me start the fire. They just saw me when I ordered you back into the building and put out the fire."

"What did the note say?"

"Ye don't want to know."

"Olin, tell me."

Olin jumped up and walked away from her. "No. It was rude and something a fine lass should not see."

"Olin." She stood up. "I will not have you treat me as a child. Give me that note."

Olin came behind her and wrapped his arms around her. His lips were mere inches from her ears. Gooseflesh rose down her neck to her arms. "Ida Mae," he whispered, "please trust me."

She twisted in his arms and faced him. "I do trust you. Please trust me. I can handle it."

He released her and stepped back. Looking down, he swept the floor with his right boot. "It was a single word meaning a lady of ill repute."

Ida Mae's nerves kicked in once again and her stomach twisted like a lemon being wrung out of all its flavor. Taking in a deep breath, she let it out slowly. "More than one saw us last night."

"Aye, I'm afraid so. Ye and the good Lord know nothing

inappropriate happened between us last night, but someone doesn't see it that way."

"Did Percy mention that?"

"No. He only knew I was moving out of the shop. He didn't even know I was moving into McGillis's Grain and Feed store."

Ida Mae paced. "Then Percy didn't throw the rock."

"No, I suppose not."

"Olin, I believe someone is out to get me. It isn't you they are after."

"Perhaps, but I believe there is more than one person behind all this. It is obvious someone didn't want me renting your father's shop. Hopefully, my move will stop that issue. Are ye up for staying in your place tomorrow night with the sheriff hiding in my shop?"

"No. . . Yes. . . I suppose I have to be. I want this to end and I want it to end now."

"Do ye know ye are beautiful when ye are determined?"

His smile melted away her anger over the situation.

"You're incorrigible."

"Aye, but that's why ye love me." He winked.

Heat blazed across her checks and down her neck. "I care, Olin. I don't know if I love."

He closed the distance between them. The touch of his fingers brushing the stray strands of hair from her face excited and calmed her all at the same time. "I care, too."

She closed her eyes, willing him to come closer and kiss her.

"May I?" he whispered.

nine

"Bobby. . ." His mother's voice skidded to a halt.

Olin's heart thumped. Ida Mae buried her face in his chest. The raw emotions mixed with the memory of her lips doubled his determination to help this woman.

"I'm sorry," his mother mumbled. She silently slipped out of the room.

Olin pulled back from Ida Mae. He gave her a wink, then called out to his mother. "Mum!"

She reentered the room. "Ye know I'm not sorry. Here ye be claimin' ye ain't in love, and what do I find? Ye young'uns best learn what love is."

Ida Mae pulled his shirt around the edges of her face.

His love for her deepened a hundredfold. "Hey, sweetheart." He nudged her chin with his forefinger. "Mum won't bite."

"Aye, I might take ye over my knee, but I won't bite ye."

Ida Mae moaned.

It took all of Olin's strength not to laugh at her embarrassment.

"Your father was on my heels. Ye best come apart or you'll be even more embarrassed."

Ida Mae released his shirt and stepped back, turning away from him, away from his mother.

"Mum, would ye excuse us for a moment?"

He took Ida Mae's hand and tugged. She resisted for a moment, then followed him out the back door. He led her to the shade tree and the swing his father had built years ago. "I'm sorry to have embarrassed you, but I'm not sorry for kissing you."

Her eyes glistened. "It was wrong."

"Why?" He sat down on the swing and patted the seat for her to join him. She continued to stand.

"Because it isn't proper. You and I haven't courted."

"Ida Mae, I'd ask yer father for your hand in marriage, but he's not here. This has to be your decision."

"Marriage? It was just a kiss."

"Was it?" He couldn't argue with her. It was simply a kiss. But the moment their lips met he knew beyond any human reason this woman was made for him, that God designed them to be together one day. She had to feel it, too.

"There's too much going on right now for me to know whether I love you or not. My emotions have gone from one extreme to another. How can I know what I'm feeling is real and not the result of all the turmoil I felt before we kissed?"

"Sweetheart, please sit with me. I promise not to kiss you unless ye ask." He wiggled his eyebrows.

Ida Mae let out a strangled laugh and joined him.

He wrapped his arm around her but didn't draw her close.

"We can hold off on marriage for a while."

"You're worse than your mother."

"Aye, I suppose I am. Before I kissed you I knew I cared for ye deeply. But when we kissed my love for you grew."

Ida Mae sighed. "I can't trust my emotions. Look what happened after the fire and my foolish trust in Cyrus. I don't know what that man is doing on my farm, but he isn't farming. I think he's found a free place to live and I let him."

What does this have to do with the kiss? "Did ye kiss Cyrus?"

"No. I mean I trusted him because of how he helped me after the fire. He took care of so many things. But he wasn't the man I thought him to be. I reckon I shouldn't have let him farm the land when I caught him and Rosey out at the farmhouse, but it made sense at the time."

"Cyrus isn't a farmer. Neither am I for that matter. But he did do an excellent job rebuilding the house, didn't he?"

"Yes."

"Don't doubt yourself, then. Ye did what was right with what facts ye knew. We now know he can't farm, so you will not let him live there again after the harvest."

"True."

"Ida Mae, I see in ye an incredible woman. Yes, I want to protect you. But ye have done well to settle your parents' accounts and work out a plan with your brothers for the family assets. You are a smart woman. Not to mention a wonderful spinster."

"Don't remind me."

"Pardon?"

"Never mind. Just my foolish ramblings about the two meanings of the word."

Spinster? Ah, one who spins and an old single lass. "I can change one of those meanings for you."

She slapped him on the knee.

"Tell me this, at least. Are ye at peace with me beside you?"

She glanced down at her hands. Her soft, delicate hands. Olin swallowed a desire to kiss each and every one of her fingers.

"Yes," she whispered.

Olin's heart soared.

The sound of a horse approaching caused him to remove his arm from around her shoulders.

❧

Ida Mae was more confused now than she was on her arrival earlier that morning. Olin had no idea how much she enjoyed and longed for another kiss from him. Even if it was just an emotional response to the shocking events of the day.

"Ida Mae?" The deep voice of her uncle, Minnie's father, echoed between the house and the barn. "Where are you?"

Olin jumped up from the swing and held out his hand to assist her. She took it but let go as soon as she was on her feet. There was no question what her uncle was here for or who told her uncle where she was. "Uncle Ty, I'm out back."

The man stood about six feet tall. "Your cousin told me I'd find you here. Come on. You're coming home with me."

"I'm fine, Uncle Ty. Have you met Olin Orr?"

"Hello, sir." Olin extended his hand.

"I ain't met him, nor do I have a mind to. You're coming home with me right now. I ain't having the whole town shaking their tongues about our family and how my niece is a lady of ill repute."

Olin's shoulders squared as he stepped in front of the man. "Ye will not speak of Ida Mae that way. Nor shall ye speak to her in that manner."

Ida Mae placed her hand on Olin's forearm. "It's all right. I'll go with him."

"Ye will not. I won't have ye subjected to such evil thoughts."

Uncle Ty paled. "What gives you the right, son?"

"I love her. And if ye did, ye wouldn't have spoke such to her."

Kyle, John, and Olin's father came out of the barn and stood beside her and Olin.

"Uncle Ty, I've done nothing wrong. Olin simply offered a place for me to stay while my window is repaired."

"And his mother and I would nay allow any improprieties in our house."

"I'll go if you insist. But at least here I have my own room and my own bed. I'm not partial to sleeping with Minnie. The girl tosses and turns all night."

Uncle Ty relaxed. "You weren't taken against your will?"

"No, sir. Olin's a perfect gentleman."

Mrs. Orr joined them, rubbing her hands on her apron. "Can I get ye a glass of iced tea?"

"That would be mighty neighborly of you. I guess I let my emotions run away with me."

Olin's father walked up to him. "I have a couple daughters of my own. I understand. Come in the house and let's set a spell."

Kyle and John went back to the barn. Olin, his parents, Uncle Ty, and Ida Mae sat down in the front sitting room. "Mighty fine house you have."

"Thank ye. The good Lord's blessed us."

Uncle Ty's house was a rugged log cabin with small rooms.

They finished off the dirt floors a few years back. He was a hard worker, and over the years Minnie spent more money than they could afford. Thankfully, they sent her to work at the local bakery a few years back and it had been a huge help.

"Ida Mae, Minnie's been tellin' us all kinds of things. Has someone been stealing from you?"

"Yes."

"And there have been broken windows?"

"Yes."

"What about this fire? Minnie said Olin's been rumored to have started it."

Mr. Orr cleared his throat.

"Forgive me; she said it was a rumor."

Olin spoke up. "Most of what Minnie has shared with you is true. For some reason folks are trying to bring up the past and make me leave town. You may speak with the sheriff and confirm his re-investigation into Gary Jones's death. I admit he died at my hands while we were involved in childish fisticuffs but it was accidental."

Ty turned to address Ida Mae. "I'm still concerned about folks thinking you are not behaving as a lady should."

"I can't do anything about gossip, and I certainly can't do anything about Minnie. She means well, but she'll listen to anything and assume it is so. As I said outside, I'll stay with you for the night if you insist, but I'd prefer to stay out here, if you don't mind. I'm returning to my home tomorrow."

"Well, I don't know. Your aunt will have my hide if I don't bring ya. But I can see that these folks will watch over you. Why don't you stay in your shop tonight, Olin?"

"I moved my shop to McGillis's Grain and Feed. There isn't room for a cot in there."

Not to mention the sheriff will be sleeping in his old shop tonight. Ida Mae smiled. "Uncle Ty, I am fine and I am safe."

"Very well. But I want you to let us know the next time."

There hadn't been time. "Sure. I'm sorry to have put you through so much worry."

Olin stood first. "Mr. Jacobs, who told Minnie that the town was gossiping about Ida Mae being a woman of ill repute?"

"I don't know. She said someone saw you entering Ida Mae's late last night."

Olin glanced over at Ida Mae.

"That was in the middle of the night."

"You mean it's true?" Ty's hands clutched the arms of his chair until his knuckles turned white.

❧

Olin had taken just about enough from Ida Mae's *caring* family. "Sir, I told ye once, ye will not speak thus to Ida Mae. I shall not warn ye a second time."

"Uncle Ty, relax, please. There was a fire outside my house. Olin put it out. We were talking in the entryway. Nothing happened."

"I ain't about to put up with the likes of you speakin' to me in such tones. Ida Mae, come with me now. Pack your bags and come."

Ida Mae stood up.

"No, she's not leaving. She's safe here and she'll stay here."

"Olin Robert Orr, sit down." His father stood with his hands on his hips and pointed toward Uncle Ty's chair.

"Mr. Jacobs, have ye ever known Ida Mae to be anything less than honorable?"

"No."

"Ye should be trustin' your niece, not the gossip of others."

Olin fought the desire to escort the man from his home. He was looking after the well-being of Ida Mae, even if it was misguided.

"On my word of honor, Mr. Jacobs, we did nothing inappropriate last night or any other time."

The sheriff and Olin had decided to keep the message from the rock hidden in hopes of exposing the person who had written it. But it appeared the individual had already started informing others. Olin wanted to be on the streets, watching Ida Mae's. He wanted to catch this man in the act.

No, he *needed* to catch this man. *Ida Mae should not live in fear or humiliation because of her relationship with me, Lord.*

"I'm sorry I spoke poorly of Ida Mae. I do apologize. I've been up all night, helping birth a calf. But it ain't right for Ida Mae to stay here when folks are suspectin' the worst. I think she should stay with us."

"I'll come." Ida Mae stood. "I'll get my carpetbag."

"Are ye sure?"

"Yes, Olin, thank you. It's for the best."

"As ye wish. I'll lend you my horse." Olin walked out to the barn.

"What's happenin'?" John and Kyle jumped on him when he entered the barn.

"She's going home with her uncle."

"I don't like it," Kyle said, twisting the rope in his hand.

"Neither do I, but it is her family and it is her choice."

"Aye, 'tis true. What should we do about the recent rock?"

"Let me give Ida Mae my horse. I'll come back and tell ye the plans."

Olin walked the horse over to the front door. He'd left it saddled when he returned from town; he'd been waiting to discuss his returning tonight to watch the street when he was pleasantly interrupted. Olin thought back on their kiss. Warmth and a huge sense of protectiveness came over him.

Ida Mae and her uncle exited the house. "Are ye sure?" he asked again, praying she'd change her mind.

"Yes."

His heart sank.

"I love ye," he whispered as he helped her mount the horse.

Ida Mae's smile sent his heart thumping again. "I'll see you in the morning, Olin."

"Aye."

"Come on, girl, the sun will be setting soon." Ty Jacobs clicked his tongue and his horse trotted forward.

Ida Mae followed.

Olin watched as they made their way down the long dirt

road. She turned back and waved just before the bend. *Please, Lord, keep her safe.*

Olin ran back to the barn. "Saddle up the horses, boys. We have a long night ahead of us."

ten

"Minnie, please stop. What is it with you?"

"Me? You're the one that won't listen to common sense. The man is dangerous, I tell you."

Ida Mae's patience was wearing thin. She would much rather be savoring the memory of Olin's kiss than arguing with her cousin that she didn't know what she was talking about. "Minnie, I don't know why you believe Percy Mandrake anyway. The man is not the most God-fearing man in the county."

"But he's fine-lookin'."

"If you say so." Olin's deep brown eyes and wonderfully curly black hair flooded back in her mind.

"See, ya know what I mean. Percy also knows how to treat a woman."

Ida Mae's smile slipped. "Minnie, I don't know Percy, but he's never struck me as being completely honest." *And how does one trust a male gossip? Not that I trust a female one, either.*

"He says Bobby has always been a problem."

"Maybe for him. Olin says ever since they were children Percy and he never got along. They've been oil and water forever."

"See, you have to agree with me. Percy is telling the truth."

"No, I don't have to agree with you. Percy is not telling the entire truth. How'd he know that Olin came into my house last night? It was the middle of the night. No one should have been out there walking the streets."

"So, why was Bobby?"

"He couldn't sleep and came by to check on me because of all the problems I've been having."

"Neighbors said he started the fire."

"And the sheriff got the truth out of them that they didn't really see him start the fire. And why does Percy want Olin out of town so badly?" Ida Mae pressed. "After all these years, why does he care? It seems to me he goes out of his way to interfere with Olin's life, and Olin hasn't done anything to Percy."

Minnie curled her knees up to her chest. "You trust Olin that much?"

"Yes. Do you trust Percy that much?" Ida Mae sat down on the bed beside her cousin and faced her.

Minnie hung her head. "No, I suppose I don't."

"Ah, so who do you think might be right in this case, Olin or Percy?"

Minnie shot her chin upward. "I'd hate to admit it, but probably Olin."

Ida Mae smiled. "Thank you. That's what I wanted to hear. Now, let's get to sleep so I can go to work having rested a little bit."

They shifted and slipped under the covers. "Ida Mae?"

"Hmm."

"Cyrus is still telling folks you and he are married."

"What?" Ida Mae shot back upright. "He's married; I'm not."

"He's married?"

Ida Mae closed her eyes and sighed. "Yes, but promise me you won't tell a single soul. I mean it, Minnie, not one person."

"Who to, if it ain't you?"

"I can't say. I promised I wouldn't. They haven't told her parents yet."

"Oh, brother. If I marry I won't be staying in my parents' house and pretending I'm not."

"Nor would I."

Ida Mae lay back down and slipped the covers over herself once again.

"Ida Mae?"

"Hmm." *Please, God, let her sleep. My nerves are shot. I need some peace.*

"Do you think you'll get married?"

"I hope to."

"I'm worried. We're getting too old. Men like the younger women."

"Minnie, trust the Lord."

"I suppose."

Ida Mae thought of a hundred things to say to her cousin about trusting the Lord and not throwing herself at men as she had in the past. Minnie rolled to her side. Ida Mae rolled to her other side and faced the dark wall. Choosing to think on better things, she allowed her mind to go back to the kitchen at the Orrs' farm. Olin's warm embrace, their tender kiss and his mother's. . . Ida Mae giggled.

"What?" Minnie whispered.

⁂

Olin sequestered himself behind the houses of the nosy neighbors who had reported him to the sheriff. They had a fair view of Ida Mae's shop. In the dark, it didn't make sense that they could have made out that it was him who put out the fire. He didn't know these people. They were new in town, at least within the past seven years. Charlotte was growing. No one could know everyone any longer.

A man walked past Ida Mae's building. It was late enough that most folks were home in bed. Olin whistled the night owl's birdsong to alert his brothers that someone was walking past.

The man continued to walk at a slow but even pace.

Olin sat for another hour until a dim light appeared in Ida Mae's room. He eased out of his cramped space and stretched his muscles. Should he go in?

He signaled Kyle with the screech owl's birdsong, which would keep John perched with a perfect shot of the back door if someone should come out.

Kyle jogged quietly among the shadows.

"Look." Olin pointed.

"Someone's in there."

"Aye, it could be the sheriff. Should I go in?"

"No, little brother, ye stay here. I'll take a wide circle around the block and sneak up to the blacksmith shop and tell the sheriff."

"Tap the door three times lightly. If he doesn't answer, barge in."

Kyle nodded and slipped back into the shadows.

Olin moved to a location closer to the back door but lay down under some overgrown bushes, praying that he wouldn't disturb any snakes or other creeping animals.

Ten minutes later a man yelled in front of the shop. Olin bolted, immediately joined by John.

&

Exhausted, Ida Mae prayed she could get some rest in her own bed. She didn't have any clients coming in this morning, so she decided to close the shop for the morning and take advantage of her own bed. Whomever Minnie married would have to snore louder than her or else be deaf, because he wouldn't get a wink of sleep otherwise. She felt some relief that her family believed her about Olin. Granted, the Jacobses were hesitant, but they did trust her. It had been a good decision to go home with Uncle Ty. She would have preferred to stay at Olin's, but her family needed to know Olin was not the man the rumors made him out to be. What still bothered her was Percy Mandrake. Why did he hold so much disdain for Olin?

"Ida Mae! Ida Mae!" Mrs. Waters ran up to her as she exited the stable. "Did you hear what happened last night?"

Dread spiraled down her spine. Olin said the sheriff was going to spend the night in the shop. "No, what happened?"

"In the middle of the night a man fell and broke his leg right in front of your shop. Can you imagine?"

"No, who?"

"Sheriff found him in the wee hours. What was the man doing out at that hour, I ask you? Up to no good, I tell you."

"He was in front of my shop?"

"Actually, by the town well, but that's just about in front of your shop. You didn't have a gentleman caller again last night, did you?"

Ida Mae held down her temper. "No. I didn't have one any other night, either, contrary to gossip."

"Where were you last night?"

"I spent the night at my uncle Ty's house with my cousin Minnie, if you must know."

"Oh, I heard you were out at the Orrs' farm."

"I visited Mrs. Orr during the day. Mr. Orr insisted I stay away from my shop while he cleaned up the damage and the sheriff investigated. Then I ate dinner and spent the night with Minnie."

"Oh. I knew you were a good girl."

"Mrs. Waters, who's been spreading ugly words about me?"

"I don't know, dear. No one seems to have seen anything, just hearsay, which is why I came to you directly."

Ida Mae smiled. "Please inform your friends I was safe with my family last night."

"I'll be happy to spread the word."

"Thank you."

Mrs. Waters left before Ida Mae remembered that she hadn't heard who got hurt in front of her shop. She unlocked the front door and went inside. Olin had cleaned up the broken glass. The window was covered by wood. It wasn't pretty but it was functional.

In her room, she flopped down on her bed.

The hammering of someone knocking and calling her name woke her up. She glanced at the clock. *Oh my.* Rattled, she jumped up and ran to the door.

"Olin, what's the matter?"

"Are you all right?"

"Yes, what's wrong?"

"Nothing now. I was worried when you didn't answer the door and I saw my horse in the stable."

"Come, come inside."

"Do you think it is wise?"

"Come, I need to speak with you privately."

Olin looked over his shoulder and walked into the shop,

leaving the door open to the street.

"Olin, my reputation is already ruined."

"Not beyond repair. Besides, I'd want to sweep you in my arms and kiss you, if it were allowed."

Heat flickered across her cheeks. "And I you. Do you know what happened last night?"

"Yes, my brothers and I," he said, dropping his voice to a whisper, "came out after a couple hours' sleep to check on the shop and the sheriff. Someone came inside. There was a low light moving in your room."

"Did you catch him?"

"No. Kyle got knocked from behind and twisted his ankle. The yell sent John and me to his side, as well as Sheriff Thatcher."

"Oh dear. Is he all right?"

"Doc says he'll be fine in a week or more, just has to keep off his leg for a while."

Ida Mae stepped toward him. Olin stepped back. "Please stay there, Ida Mae. I want to hold ye so bad I ache.

"The sheriff has a plan," he continued. "As you recall, the sheriff wants ye to stay here tonight, but he'll be here, as well. He's ordered the locks changed on your door, and that will be taken care of later today. Whoever it is has a key—or knows how to pick a lock like me. Either way, the sheriff will be staying with you, as will his wife. He wants everyone to know he's looking after you. He's hoping that will be enough to scare this man off."

"I'm scared, Olin."

&

Olin couldn't take it any longer. He closed the door with the heel of his boot and wrapped her in his arms. "I know, sweetheart, but it will be all right. We figure whoever it is, is coming late at night. That gives me time to go home and sneak back into town unnoticed. I'll be in the shop tonight, too, but we don't want anyone knowing that."

She trembled in his arms.

"This will be over soon, Ida Mae. It has to be."

He didn't have the heart to tell her they now suspected more than one person. Whoever was inside couldn't have knocked Kyle down.

"Ida Mae?" Minnie rushed through the door. "What are you doing? Get your hands off of her this minute." Minnie swatted Olin with her purse.

Olin blocked her blows with his arm.

"Minnie, stop." Ida Mae wiped the tears from her eyes. "Olin was just giving me some comfort."

"I bet."

"I'll be back, Ida Mae. Good day, Miss Jacobs."

Olin heard Minnie rush up to Ida Mae, asking her what happened.

The rest of the day went well. He worked on the few orders he had and on Mr. Bechtler's request. He'd formed other molds before, but this one would be the first he'd ever made for a gold coin. And it was still a secret. He tapped the mold into a piece of tin. He still had work to do, but it was coming. He flattened the impression in the tin so no one would know what he had been working on. His privacy in this small shop was limited. Carrying Mr. Bechtler's design back and forth with him each night gave him some security that it would not fall into the wrong hands.

Each evening nothing happened. The sheriff felt fairly confident Ida Mae was now safe.

ॐ

Five days later everything seemed back to normal, except for Olin's growing attraction to Ida Mae. They were deliberately meeting one another in public places, being kind and cordial with one another, denying their true feelings, and otherwise keeping their distance. If Ida Mae was as half torn up about it as he was, she was hurting, too. He'd sent his mother in to invite her to dinner so they could have some alone time. John met them at the end of the day and escorted them back to the farm.

"Ye are causing a heap of trouble, little brother."

"Thanks for coming out, John."

"Ye are welcome. How are ye, Ida Mae?"

"Fine. The gossip is winding down about me so the shop is starting to pick up a bit."

"I'm glad to hear it."

As they left the outskirts of town John pulled his horse away from them. "How are ye really?" Olin asked.

"Better. I'm sleeping again."

"Good."

"How are you?"

"About ready to climb the walls if I can't be with you real soon. I miss ye so much."

Ida Mae giggled. "I miss you, too. How can that be?"

"Ah, me sweetheart, 'tis love." He wiggled his eyebrows for her.

"How's Kyle?"

"Grumpier than a bear woken from his winter slumber. But he's walking around a bit. Thankfully, the work is lighter around the farm right now.

"Have you heard anything from Cyrus? How the farm is doing?"

"No, and I'm not asking, either. Every time I go to deal with him the situation looks bleaker. I reckon this will not be an income-producing year. Any profits will go to my brothers."

"I thought the will was settled."

"It is, and the property is mine. But I want to give them a share of the profits for the next five years if I keep the farm. If not, I'll sell and divide the monies between us."

"You don't have to according to the will, right?"

"True, but I want to."

Olin smiled. This was the woman he loved. "I love your generous heart, Ida Mae."

When they arrived at the farm Olin helped Ida Mae off the horse. She went inside while he and John put the horses in the barn.

"Is she spending the night?" John asked.

"I'd feel better if she did. But I don't think it would be wise for her reputation."

"Aye, ye are probably correct. Can ye give me a hand after dinner? It won't take but a half hour. It needs two sets of strong hands, and Dad's been workin' hard, covering for Kyle's share."

"Be happy to."

"Oh, bring a rifle with you tonight. I saw bear tracks today."

With all the things Olin had to worry about he didn't want to add one more. He knew it seemed that the danger was past for Ida Mae, but something he couldn't quite figure out was still nagging him about the night Kyle got hurt.

A shiver sliced down his spine. If a man would hurt Kyle for no reason, what would he do to Ida Mae?

eleven

Ida Mae's heart warmed at Olin's touch as he wrapped his fingers around hers. "Come with me."

She couldn't remember a more pleasant evening. For the past thirty minutes she'd sat and read while Mrs. Orr played her piano and Mr. Orr read a book. Olin had been gone for nearly a half hour. She'd forgotten what it was like to be a part of a real family, and she ached to have it once again.

"Olin, I don't want to leave."

Olin wrapped his arms around her. "I'm just taking ye to the backyard to sit on the swing. The stars are beautiful tonight."

"I don't want to go home tonight. Can I stay in the spare room?"

"Ye need to go home, and soon. John and Father will be riding with us tonight. We're not takin' any chances."

"Then we should leave now. I don't want to keep your family up late."

"We can have a few minutes," he whispered. "Alone."

Gooseflesh tingled all over. "Kiss me, before I faint."

Olin chuckled. "Remember, I said I wouldn't kiss ye until ye asked. Thankfully, ye finally asked."

He captured her lips with a hunger that met her own. It had been nearly a full week since their first kiss and, oh, did she love kissing this man. She threaded her fingers through his silky hair. "I've missed you."

"I've missed ye as well. Will ye marry me now?"

"Olin, we can't."

"Why not?"

Why not? she wondered. "Because we have so much to learn about each other first."

"We can learn it married."

"Olin, you're impossible."

"I believe ye said incorrigible before."

She wrapped him in her arms and held on to him. She didn't want to leave. She didn't want to return to a life alone in her shop. She wanted what he had, wanted what his family had. "Where would we live?"

"Is that a yes?"

"No, it's a curious question. My room isn't big enough for two."

"My room isn't big enough for two here." He stepped away from her. "Before all these strange events I was determined to have a certain income, and a house, before I asked a woman to marry me. Now, all I can think about is you, and being by your side without fear of shaming ye."

"Olin, I do love you. But the time isn't right for us to marry."

"Aye, ye speak the truth, lass. But mark my words, we will marry."

"Aye," she agreed, mimicking his brogue.

Olin roared. "I love ye more than words can say, Ida Mae. Come, let's sit for a spell before we have to bring you home."

Ida Mae snuggled beside him on the swing. They rocked back and forth without saying a word and just relaxed in each other's arms. The stars sparkled against the black velvet sky. The fresh smell of cut grass seemed richer, more vibrant. Life felt better in Olin's arms. *Yes, I will marry you, Olin Robert Orr.*

"Olin, Ida Mae, it's time to be goin'!" Mrs. Orr called out.

છે

They rode with lanterns burning, giving them a clearer path in the dark. Olin knew the roads well enough that lanterns weren't necessary, but for safety they felt it best to use them.

Olin walked Ida Mae to her door. His heart jumped in his chest when he saw it. He pulled Ida Mae back to the horses. "John, get the sheriff."

"What's wrong?"

"I'm not sure, but there is blood all over the front door. Let's not stir up attention. Move the animals to Ida Mae's father's shop and stable."

"I should check my place." Ida Mae took a step forward.

"No, honey, please. Stay with my father. I'll check everything out."

"All right."

After he had his father and Ida Mae settled in the blacksmith shop, he slipped into Ida Mae's shop through the secret door, still open as the sheriff had requested. As his eyes adjusted to the light of the lantern, he saw that nothing appeared out of place.

There was a knock at the door.

"Evenin', Sheriff."

"What happened here?"

"I don't know. There's blood all over the front door."

"Chicken or pig, I suspect. Is there a note?"

"Not that I've spotted so far. Father and Ida Mae are in her father's shop. I came in through the secret passageway."

The sheriff slipped his hat up his forehead. "I guess this isn't over."

"No, and I don't want Ida Mae staying here. It isn't safe."

"What do you suggest?"

"I don't know. I could bring her back home tonight."

"Someone must have known you were taking her home tonight. Doesn't this fellow usually come later in the evening?"

"Change of pattern?"

"More than likely. Let me look over the shop and Ida Mae's room. I'll meet you in McAuley's blacksmith shop."

"Yes, sir." Olin couldn't wait to be with Ida Mae.

"When the sheriff comes we're going to pack up some clothes and bring ye to our house."

"What was in there, son?"

"Nothing, all looks normal to me. But the sheriff knows what to look for."

"Aye, he's a good man. Ida Mae, ye are welcome to our home for as long as ye wish."

Olin winked. Ida Mae smiled.

The sheriff slipped through the secret doorway. "Hello, Miss McAuley. How are you?"

"Terrified."

"You should be. I don't know what's going on, but I think you'll be safer at the Orrs' farm." The sheriff started looking around to see if anything had been disturbed in the smithy.

He opened a cabinet door toward the front of the smithy that was slightly ajar and Olin blinked. "Where did that come from?"

"Ida Mae, please come here," Sheriff Thatcher ordered. "Are these the items that were missing from your room and shop?"

Even Olin recognized some of the items from the descriptions Ida Mae had given him before.

"Yes. Olin, why are they here?"

"I didn't put them here."

"Shh, relax, everyone. I believe someone is trying to have Olin blamed for all the missing items. Let's leave them here for now. Whoever stole the items wants them to be discovered. If Olin had taken these, he wouldn't have left them where customers could see them when he opened the cupboard. What concerns me is that the intruder now has a new key or has learned to pick locks like Olin."

"You can pick a lock?" John questioned.

Olin nodded.

"If I'd known that I'd have had ye open a trunk I lost the key to two years ago," John chuckled.

"Olin, take Ida Mae home. Tonight I'll need one of you to stay up all night or to work in shifts, but I want someone to watch over your home just in case. The blood on the front door is a more desperate warning."

"Sheriff, me boys and I will take care of Ida Mae and our own. Ye can count on us."

"Thank you, Mr. Orr." The sheriff extended his hand. "I'll ride out in the morning and tell you what I find."

Olin escorted Ida Mae to her horse. She was shaking now. The shock was setting in. "I'll ride Ida Mae with me. We'll leave her horse here. She's too shaky to ride alone in the dark."

Ida Mae nodded.

They removed her horse's gear and set him up with some fresh oats and water.

The sheriff stepped back through the secret door. John slipped out of the shop first, then Olin and Ida Mae, followed by his father. They kept the lanterns off until they reached the end of town.

"We forgot to pack her clothes."

"Your mother will fix her up, son. Let's get home. It's too late to stay out here."

Olin couldn't agree more.

John lifted his rifle.

ے

Ida Mae buried her head in Olin's back. *Blood! Blood on my door! Why, Lord?* Ida Mae prayed for understanding. What had she done to make someone so upset with her? Or was it that someone was so upset with Olin that they would go to such extreme lengths to have him blamed for all the weird happenings at her shop? It didn't make sense. Nothing made sense, except for her oneness with Olin. He'd been right; they should marry. They were meant for one another. He completed her in so many ways. All the unanswered questions in her life seemed to be answered, or at least calmed, by his presence. Yes, she loved Olin Orr, and she would be honored to be his wife. But would life allow it?

She held him tighter. He patted her hands. "It'll be all right, Ida Mae. With God's grace we'll get through this. I love ye, sweetheart."

By the time they arrived at the house and got Ida Mae set up in the spare room, everyone was exhausted. Kyle said he'd take the first watch. Olin would get up in two hours and watch until five. Then John would get up and watch for a half hour until Mr. Orr would get up, then John would get the morning chores under way. Ida Mae didn't think she could sleep, but the moment her head hit the feather pillow she was dreaming of living the rest of her life in Olin's arms.

࿇

When the cock crowed for the third time, Ida Mae pushed herself out of bed. The smell of frying bacon drew her to the kitchen. Due to the lateness of the hour the night before, she'd received only sleeping garments from Mrs. Orr. As quickly as possible, she dressed in her own clothes before entering the kitchen for breakfast.

"Good morning, Ida Mae. Would you like some coffee or tea?"

"Coffee, if you don't mind."

"Coffee it is." Mrs. Orr poured her a cup and set it down on the small kitchen table.

"Is there anything I can do to help?"

Mrs. Orr smiled. "No, thank you. I've been in a rhythm for years."

"I understand." Ida Mae sipped the rich brew. Coffee would help dissolve the cobwebs in her brain.

"We're having eggs, bacon, grits, and blueberries this morning. Is that all right with ye?"

"I haven't eaten a full breakfast like that in over a year."

"And I daresay it shows. Ye are nothing but skin and bones."

"I've always been on the slight side. But I haven't eaten as well since my parents died. It's hard to cook for one."

"Aye, I can imagine. Ye will fill your belly this mornin'." She went back to frying up the bacon on the woodstove. "I tend to use the summer kitchen outside during these warm months, but I didn't want to have ye leavin' the house this mornin' in case anyone is watching."

"I appreciate that."

"Aye. A dip in the stream might be in order today. I could use a good scrubbin'. How about you?"

"Yes, I could use one as well."

"I'll find ye some clean clothes after breakfast. We'll have Mr. Orr join us for the bath."

Ida Mae nearly dropped her cup of coffee.

"Forgive me. He'll join us with his shotgun and keep watch

over the swimming hole. He won't be bathing with us."

Ida Mae's cheeks flamed. Of course, Mrs. Orr was thinking of their safety.

The men came in from the morning chores, and breakfast was consumed faster than Mrs. Orr could cook it. "I've been thinkin'," Kyle said, breaking off another piece of bread to scoop up his eggs. "Since ye and Ida Mae will be gettin' married, why don't ye do it now?"

Ida Mae choked on her eggs.

Mrs. Orr slapped her back.

Mr. Orr coughed.

"What?" John shook his head.

Olin slipped down in his chair.

John reached across the table and grabbed the platter of bacon. "Kyle, you don't just get married to keep a woman safe."

"I know that. But I heard them talking about it last night."

All eyes turned to Olin and then back to Ida Mae.

Olin was at least as red as she was.

"Son?"

Olin cleared his throat and pulled at his open collar.

Ida Mae giggled. She couldn't stop it, try as she might. It didn't take long for Mrs. Orr to join her, then Mr. Orr, John, and Kyle. Olin was the last to laugh. "Aye, Ida Mae and I are talking 'bout getting married," he admitted amid the laughter.

"Congratulations, little brother." John slapped him on the back. "I can't believe ye will make it to the altar before me."

Olin grinned.

"And welcome to the family, Ida Mae."

"It's about time I had another lady around." Mrs. Orr got up and kissed her on the cheek. "Ye be makin' a good choice, son."

"Back to my question, so why don't ye?"

The front door knocker resounded through the room. "That must be Sheriff Thatcher." Olin excused himself and went to the front door.

Should we marry now?

twelve

"Good morning, Sheriff. What did ye find?"

"I'm concerned, Olin. Can we talk outside for a minute?"

"Sure." Olin shut the door behind him. "What's the matter?"

"I truly fear someone is trying to set you up, but I fear it is something far worse than stealing trinket items from Ida Mae. It doesn't add up that someone would be so upset with Ida Mae. She's done nothing wrong to anyone, intentionally or otherwise."

"I agree. And the town has been full of gossip regarding my return. I should have stayed in the north."

"Perhaps, but if we are dealing with someone so evil he would frame another man for acts of self-defense done in years past, I'm glad to know it now rather than later when it might be too late."

Olin didn't know if he agreed with that thought or not. He loved Ida Mae and wouldn't want to be the cause of all this bad will toward her, and yet he was. How could he possibly ask her to marry him with that kind of a stigma over them the rest of their lives? It just wouldn't be fair. "I can leave town in a couple days."

John Thatcher scratched his unshaved chin. "No, that's not what I had in mind. When I got up this morning the town was buzzing that someone killed Ida Mae and carried her body off. Apparently, three horsemen were seen leaving the town last night and one looked to be carrying a body."

"I think we should include Ida Mae in this discussion."

"We will in just a moment. What I want to suggest is a bit unorthodox, but I believe it might bring our enemy out of hiding. I'm suggesting we go along with the rumors."

"Pardon?" Olin rubbed the wax from his ears. The sheriff

couldn't possibly have said what he thought he said.

"What I'm suggesting is we let folks believe she is dead."

Olin shook his head from side to side. "Ida Mae has to hear this."

Olin ushered the sheriff into the dining area where his mother quickly put a place setting in front of him. The sheriff explained to all of them what he had just explained to Olin. The room was silent.

Ida Mae opened her mouth, then closed it. Then opened it again. "Are you suggesting I pretend to be dead?"

"Yes. I can even go as far as putting out an arrest warrant for Olin."

"Thanks," Olin snickered. "I wouldn't want it in the records that I was accused of killing my wife."

"Your wife? When did you two get hitched?"

Ida Mae blushed for the second time this morning. Olin loved the playful shade of pink on her cheeks.

"We're going to get married. I'm thinking in the future."

"O–oh," Sheriff Thatcher stuttered. "Congratulations."

Olin's father got up. "I don't fancy lying to folks, but I'll mislead some to keep this young woman safe." He lifted his plate from the table. "Unfortunately, I have a farm to run and livestock to take care of. Olin, fill me in on what you decide before you go to work this morning."

"Yes, sir."

Kyle and John got up from the table and took their plates to the kitchen.

"Ida Mae, what do you think?" The sheriff forked some eggs and lifted them to his mouth. Olin had lost his appetite.

"I'll go missing for a while. If you think that will help."

"I can't promise it will, but I'm praying. Plus, you'll be safer if no one knows where you are. Even me."

"Olin?"

"Yes, Mum?"

"Ye say you've asked Ida Mae to marry ye?"

"Yes, ma'am."

"Ida Mae, ye say ye love my son?"

"Yes, ma'am."

His mother nodded slowly. "Sheriff, ye can finish your meal. But we'll take it from here. Don't be surprised if ye hear rumors that Bobby, pardon me, Olin, has captured and run off with Ida Mae."

Sheriff Thatcher lifted up his hands. "Don't tell me any more."

❧

A few hours later, Ida Mae was washing in the river beside her future mother-in-law. How life could turn around in a few short minutes could be an understatement for the past several weeks. Mrs. Orr sent Olin to town to sneak in and fetch some of Ida Mae's clothes. They were going to go on the run, but not until the middle of the night. John had been sent over to the next county to bring a minister home to marry Ida Mae and Olin. Tonight she'd be a bride, a bride on the run. It wasn't exactly the way she'd pictured entering into a marriage.

Kyle had been sent to the old farmhouse on the property to clean up the place for their wedding night. It all seemed too controlled and out of her control. *I can't do this, Lord.*

"Are ye all right, dear?"

"Nervous."

"All women, and men for that matter, are nervous on their wedding day."

"This isn't the kind of wedding I dreamed about."

"No, I daresay it wouldn't be. But it will keep ye safe."

I suppose.

"Ye do love him, don't ye?"

"Yes but. . ."

"Ah, it is still too new."

"Yes."

"Answer me this: When ye kiss him, do ye feel one with him?"

"Yes."

"Then ye are meant to be together. The Lord will bless ye even if ye don't marry in a church."

"I know but. . ."

"Ye don't have to marry him. It was only a suggestion."

And a reasonable one, given all that is going on. It would be safer for us to hide as a married couple than to be alone together day and night and not be married. "It's a good plan."

Ida Mae lathered her hair. Mrs. Orr had brought her special lavender-scented soap down to the river for them to bathe with. Mr. Orr kept his back to them but kept a watchful eye around the farm.

Lord, bless this family for all they are sacrificing for me. They don't know me and yet they've taken me in as one of their own even before they knew Olin and I wanted to marry. Bless them, Lord.

Ida Mae rinsed her hair.

"Come on, dear. We've got a lot to do."

And for the rest of the day Ida Mae found herself packing and repacking. At one point she and Olin were going to take his wagon. Then it was decided that it would be too easy to track, so they would go on horseback. A pack mule was discussed, but no one had one or knew of one they could obtain without raising suspicions.

Finally, the dinner hour had arrived and Olin came home. She did love him, but she still had huge doubts about their getting married in such a manner and so soon. John returned with a preacher a few minutes later. Kyle came in needing a bath, and left as soon as he grabbed some soap and a towel.

Mrs. Orr somehow managed to prepare a huge feast for their dinner. Olin sat down at the table beside Ida Mae. He reached over and held her hand. Just touching him calmed her nerves, but was it enough?

"How is it in town?" Mr. Orr asked after saying the blessing.

Dishes passed from one to the next. Ida Mae did her best to keep up.

"Buzzing about what happened at the spinner's shop."

It was painfully obvious Olin didn't want to discuss details in front of the parson.

"I see."

"What happened in Charlotte?" Parson White asked.

"There was blood all over the door of the spinner's shop."

"That is rather strange news. I can see why everyone is talking. Is the spinster all right?"

"Yes, I am." Ida Mae spoke up. "We're not sure what happened." Olin narrowed his gaze, scrutinizing her. Ida Mae straightened in her chair.

"Do they suspect Indians?" the parson asked.

"No. But no one is quite sure who did this, or why." Olin squeezed her hand.

"We must pray for your safety. Are you certain you want to marry at this time?"

☙

Olin didn't like marrying Ida Mae under these circumstances, nor did he like hearing the rash talk all over town. Many had given him a harsh stare today. And he still wasn't settled on running off to the mountains to hide from whoever was after Ida Mae. Keeping her here on the farm seemed more prudent. But Sheriff Thatcher had a point that they could be putting his family in danger if he kept her here.

The one positive in all of this was marrying Ida Mae. It was rather soon, but he'd seen and heard many a story where a young couple married quickly and were still happily married many years later. He caressed the top of her hand with his thumb.

"Ye best stop holdin' hands and eat," Mum instructed with a tease to her voice.

Ida Mae released his hand the moment Mum spoke, and picked up her fork. He did the same.

Ida Mae's hand shook.

Father, give her strength, Olin silently prayed for her.

They made it through dinner, but Ida Mae had hardly eaten anything. She just swirled her food around her plate. Olin couldn't blame her, but he began to worry. Something was wrong.

"Shall we?" Father stood up from the table.

Mother led them all to the front parlor. The parson opened his black Bible and the pages crinkled as he turned them.

Olin took Ida Mae's hand and walked up to the parson.

"We are gathered tonight to join this man and this woman in holy matrimony. It's an honorable estate, not to be taken lightly, but reverently. . ."

Ida Mae's entire body trembled.

"What's wrong, child?" the parson asked. "Are you being forced to marry this man?"

"No."

"Are you prepared to marry him?"

She implored him with her gaze. Her brilliant blue eyes filled with tears.

"Sweetheart?" Olin reached up and caressed her face.

"I can't; I'm sorry." Ida Mae ran from the room and up the stairs.

Olin found himself a twister of emotions. He respected her if she wasn't sure, but he also felt the sting of rejection. "Forgive us, Parson White." Olin reached into his pocket. "Here's a little something for your troubles."

"Shall I stay for a bit in case the young lady changes her mind? On the other hand, the business with her front door sounds very compelling for her to want to wait."

"Let me talk with her," Mum offered and scurried off.

Olin felt helpless and dejected. For too long he'd been fighting the emotions of all the people who found fault with his return to the area. Mayhap it was best he and Ida Mae not marry. He would only ruin her and her reputation.

"Excuse me," Olin said, extricating himself from the room and going out to the barn. He kicked a clump of hay and fought the desire to punch the wall with his fist. He'd done that when he was younger and trying to control his temper. In the end, he had broken his hand.

"Wanna talk?" John asked, leaning against the door frame.

"Nothing to say. She's not ready."

"Aye, that is likely the case. But ye are takin' it rather hard if ye understand that."

Olin sighed. "She's probably right. I would only ruin her life."

"Bobby, sit down, please." John came beside him and sat down on the bale of hay. "When ye came home I didn't know you. But I watched, and ye are a good and honorable man. Pa is real proud of ye. Mum is, too, but ye know Mum—she's proud of us no matter what. And Ida Mae adores you. I know, I've watched her and you when ye were together."

"The feeling is mutual."

"Aye, I seen that, too. A man never looked more smitten than ye."

"What do we do about the plan?"

"I still agree you need to take her into hiding. How many are accusing you of harming Ida Mae?"

"No one said anything directly to me, but I'm certain the sheriff got an ear full."

"Don't be too sure. I've been giving this a lot of thought. Percy has been on a rampage since you returned. He has no interest in Ida Mae, but he does want to see ye fall for whatever reason."

"True."

"And, I'm not certain but I think I saw one of Ida Mae's customers sneaking behind her building one night while I was watching. I forget his name, but he still lives with his mother."

Olin crossed his arms. "So do we."

"Aye, but I think this man has eyes for Ida Mae."

"But to go to that extreme—pouring chicken blood on her door—it still doesn't make sense."

"They figured out what kind of animal blood?"

"Aye, Sheriff Thatcher had the butcher check it out."

"That would narrow it down some. Whoever it is has to have access to a fair amount of chickens."

"Sheriff's been checking with all the farms to see if anyone is missing any or has quite a few draining."

"He seems like a smart man. I think ye still need to take Ida Mae out of here. I know ye won't be married, and it could have a negative effect on her reputation, but I'd rather that than her not being alive."

"True. I just don't want to push her too hard."

John let out a nervous chuckle. "Let's see, ye asked the woman to marry ye after ye kissed her for the first time, and yet ye don't want to push. I've been waiting on a gal for a year now and I'm just about ready to ask her out."

"Really? Who is she?"

"I'm not telling unless she says yes." John smiled. "Some women take time. Ida Mae trusts ye, let her move at her own pace."

"Thank ye. I appreciate the advice."

"Welcome. Should I go in and tell the parson he can go home?"

"Yes, unless Ida Mae changed her mind."

"All right. Have a few words with the Lord and come and join the family. Oh, and I saw that restraint ye showed not punching that post. I'd say you've learned to control your temper."

Have I?

thirteen

"Ida Mae, may I come in?"

She sniffled and walked over to the door. Taking in a deep breath, she eased it open.

"What's the matter, dear?"

"I can't go through with it. I love him, but it's too soon. My life has been turned upside down and I don't know what to do."

"Ah, 'tis my fault for sure. Let me call down and tell the parson he can leave. Then we can have some girl talk." Mrs. Orr left.

Ida Mae didn't know if she was up to girl talk at the moment. Fear that someone was after her had spun around her heart so tight she could hardly breathe.

She scanned her packed carpetbag. Tonight could have been her wedding night. Why couldn't she go through with it? *Why? Why? Why? Lord. I don't understand. I love him but. . .*

"Please forgive me, Ida Mae, I meant no harm tryin' to push ye and Olin Robert to marry."

"It's not your fault. I should have spoken earlier."

Mrs. Orr settled down on the bed beside her. "It will be all right, dear. The good Lord will see ye through. And I do believe ye will be my daughter one day."

"Why would you want me with all the trouble I've caused this family?"

"Nonsense. 'Tis not ye that has caused the problems. It is a sinner and his sin, not you."

Ida Mae closed her eyes. She tried once again to figure out who would want to harm her.

"Ida Mae, ye are always welcome in our home."

"Thank you."

"I'll give ye some time alone." Mrs. Orr leaned into her and hugged her. "Forgive me, child. I didn't mean to add to your confusion."

"You are forgiven." Ida Mae squeezed her future mother-in-law, hoping she still would be.

When Olin's mother left the room she closed the door behind her. Ida Mae collapsed onto her pillow. Gentle tears flowed from her eyes. She shouldn't marry Olin this way. Not under such trying circumstances. If she'd gone through with the marriage tonight she would never feel confident in her own love for Olin. She needed more time. They needed more time.

Ida Mae wiped the tears from her eyes. She still needed to go into hiding, which would have been simpler if she had married Olin.

A purple glow from the setting sun filled the room. Rays of peace calmed her. She could face Olin's family even in her shame, and together they would need to amend their plans. She could go into hiding herself. She knew enough to survive for a few days. But, admittedly, she didn't know how to track or hide her own tracks. She was a farm girl who had worked in town for years. She knew her way around a spinning wheel, but she'd simply be spinning air, wandering alone in the foothills, and be an easy target if someone should try to come after her.

Composing herself, Ida Mae grabbed her carpetbag and went downstairs. Mr. Orr was reading, Olin was pacing with his back to her, and Mrs. Orr was washing dishes in the kitchen. "Olin?"

"Ida Mae." He scooped her in his arms. "Are ye all right?"

"I'm sorry."

"I understand. We'll get married sometime in the future. I can wait."

"You're not mad?"

"No, we were bending the metal before it reached its pliable point."

"I do love you." She rested her head on his shoulder. His hands caressed her hair.

"And I, ye. Come, we must decide what to do next."

"Yes. I can hide in the forest for a day or two. But I don't know how to hide my tracks. I can try—"

"I think it best if I'm with ye."

"I agree." Mr. Orr closed his book and leaned forward.

Mrs. Orr came in drying her hands on a dish towel. "So do I."

Kyle burst through the front door. "Olin, Ida Mae, the town is sending out a search party. They're organizing without the sheriff. We need to hide ye fast."

"The root cellar," Mrs. Orr offered.

"They'll search there, Mother. Can ye make it to the cabin on foot?"

"I believe so." Olin held Ida Mae's hand, then bent down and fetched a handful of ash. "Do ye trust me?"

⁂

Olin held the cold ash in his hand. He hated to do it, but if the townsfolk were close on Kyle's heels there was little choice.

Her eyes widened when she saw the ash. She nodded.

"I'm sorry." He dumped the ash in her hair and streaked her face. Then did the same to his face and hands.

"Come on. John, meet me an hour before dawn at the old parson's-nose tree and bring our bags."

His mother wrapped them in a hug. "Be off with the good Lord's blessing."

"And to think I bathed for this."

Olin laughed. He placed a bedroll and small pack over his shoulder that he had prepared earlier. "It will protect us from the full moon."

"And will I have a chance to bathe tomorrow?"

"Aye, if we are successful tonight. Come, we mustn't wait a moment longer."

Olin tugged and Ida Mae kept his pace. They ran through the back field, using the house and the barn as a cover. The wide-open field offered little protection. Olin ran toward the tree line as fast as he felt she could run. Once they hit the tree line he stopped behind a tree.

"Are we going to the cabin?"

"Not tonight. I don't know who is heading up the search party, but ye can be certain Percy is with 'em, and if he is, he knows about the old cottage. Unfortunately Kyle cleaned it up for us today so it will appear that we have stayed or are staying there. Or at least me, if they think I killed ye."

"Killed me? Why would they think that?"

"The blood. It doesn't matter that the sheriff found it to be chicken blood, not in the minds of these men. Truth is of little importance once a man makes up his mind that he is right."

Olin felt the worst decision he'd made was to come back home. And yet, having met Ida Mae and wanting to spend the rest of his life with her was a direct response to that decision. Was it wrong? Did the Lord want him here for this time and this place?

"I'm sorry, Olin."

"What for?"

She snickered. "For so many things, really. For the wedding that didn't happen, for the trouble with the shop, and for you being blamed for all of this. It's like you said before, it doesn't make sense. I can't understand why someone would want me dead or out of the way. Even to tell me to get rid of you as a tenant does not explain the chicken blood. You had moved out. The entire town knew that."

"Ah, but remember the gossip says that I ruined ye the other night. Perhaps ye have a man who fancies himself as yours. Do ye?"

"No." She cupped her face with her hands. "Only you," she muttered.

The distant sound of horses arriving at his parents' house jolted Olin back to the moment. "Come, I know a small spot where we can hide."

Olin pushed the thick brush away with his hands and held

it back until Ida Mae passed. He eased the branches back as easily as possible, trying not to disturb or break any of them. He then fluffed the underbrush behind her to keep it from appearing disturbed.

Slowly they worked their way back into the woods. He followed as many deer paths as possible. An hour later they were at the mouth of a shallow cave he had played in as a boy. He had no memory of Percy ever coming to this place, but his brothers knew where it was. And Percy, being a cousin, would probably have an idea. "Come in here."

"It doesn't look inviting."

Olin eyed the small cave. "Would ye like me to go in first?"

"Uh, does a tin man have tin?"

Olin smiled. "Not at the moment." He slipped into the dark cavern. It seemed much smaller than he remembered. He sniffed the air. It appeared stale but dry, which would make it a much more comfortable night. He lowered the bedroll and removed his flint and steel. Feeling his way along the floor he found the old campfire site and prayed that the small pile of kindling he'd always kept there as a child remained. Thankfully, it was, and extremely dry. It lit instantly as he started a small fire. He laid out the bedroll.

"Wow, I thought you said this was small."

"It is, but it's big enough to give us some protection from the night. Ida Mae, sit here. I'll be back as soon as I can. Let the fire burn out. There isn't enough wood to keep it going. I'll go gather some wood. We should be safe here for the night."

"All right."

Olin kissed her stained lips. "I'll try to be back soon. But if I'm not back by morning, go to my parents' house. Do you think you can find it?"

"No." Her voice trembled.

"It won't matter, ye'll be safe with me."

"Where's the parson's-nose tree? And why'd you name it that?"

"The parson's nose is just another name for the tail on a plucked turkey. When ye see the tree stump, you'll understand."

❧

The fatty end of the turkey's tail had been a favorite of her father's. "Do you have to leave?"

"I wanted to get some wood for a fire."

"I'm not cold." *Terrified, but not cold.*

"Yet," he added.

She reached out and held his hand, caressing it with her thumb. "Please, don't leave me alone."

"Sweetheart, I shall return."

"Do we really need a fire tonight?"

He sat down beside her. "I suppose not. Ye might get cold later."

I'm being foolish. "Olin, I'm afraid."

He wrapped his arm around her. "Ye will be safe with me."

"How can you know that? There are no guarantees in this world. Father and Mother. . ." She let her words trail off. He still had both his parents. He didn't know what it was like to lose someone so close. The past twelve months had been an agony she prayed she would never go through again. And yet the idea that someone would be after her— She felt like Job.

Olin held her tighter. "Tell me, what happened?"

"There ain't much to tell. I had to work late the night they died, so they returned home and I planned on sleeping at the shop. A fire caught in the kitchen and quickly consumed the house. The sheriff found my parents' remains in the kitchen." She paused. Olin waited while she collected her thoughts, then continued. "As best as the sheriff could tell, they were trying to put out the fire and were overtaken by the smoke."

"Did they cook often inside the house in the summer?"

"No, Mother rarely cooked more than once or twice a week at home. Since we spent so much time at the shops, she tended to cook meals there. On the weekends we'd cook the roasts or chickens. Then she'd make meals from the leftovers. We smoked a lot of our meat, so we had cured ham and bacon whenever we needed it."

That was one of the pieces of the puzzle that had made little sense to her. Why were they in the kitchen and why was Mother cooking?

"And the sheriff concluded it was an accident?"

"Yes." Ida Mae wrung the hem of her dress. "My birthday was a few days away. The sheriff thought she might have been making me a cake or something."

"Your mum made cakes in the summer for ye?"

Ida Mae giggled. She saw the same glee in his eyes that children showed in the past when her mother made a special birthday cake in the heat of the summer. Mother had said it didn't make the kitchen all that much hotter. But it had. And she loved that about her mother and father, and how they loved indulging their little girl. "I was spoiled."

"Aye, that may be an understatement. Mum uses the outdoor kitchen in the summer, but apart from bread making, she seldom fires up the oven hot enough to make baked goods, certainly not sweets."

"I was blessed."

"Ye still are, Ida Mae. Ye have all the memories, all that love, and ye are a special person. What about your brothers?"

"Randall's love is the city life and the sea. He's working in Savannah for one of the cotton shippers. His family is quite content there. Last I heard he was considering buying a plantation. But I know Randall—he'll hire someone to run it. He never liked getting his fingernails dirty. Bryan enjoyed working the land but he wanted to raise cattle, so he moved farther west to Kentucky to purchase a larger lot of land. Father sold half the farmland and gave Bryan the money for his future. He also gave a smaller share to Randall. Randall and I own the greater share in the farm. But Randall isn't interested in farming or concerned with whether I make a profit from the land. He's more concerned with his own job and how well it supports his family."

"As ye know, I, bein' the third son, inherit only a few acres of my father's property. I wanted him to give it to my brothers but Father wouldn't hear of it. So, someplace on my parents' farm I have ten acres."

Rolling her shoulders, she leaned back in a more relaxed position. "Do you know the law regarding women and their land?"

"No, not really. Why do you ask?"

"I once feared you might be after my property."

He leaned back and rested on his elbows. "What's this law say?"

"When a woman who owns property marries, the husband takes responsibility for taking care of the financial matters. He can't sell the property without her blessing, but he can do everything else. And with regard to the farm, he would have complete control over the running of it."

"Interesting."

fourteen

Olin slipped out from Ida Mae's embrace. The gentle purr signaled that he hadn't woken her. Outside, the sky was still black. He slipped through the bushes and found the deer path toward parson's-nose. John would be late doing his chores today, but not too late. By the time he reached the strangely shaped tree trunk, a small ribbon of deep blue showed on the eastern horizon.

"Mornin'," John said and wiped off the backside of his trousers. "How'd ye make out last night?"

"Fine. We spent the night in the old cave on the northeast corner."

John nodded. "Smaller, ain't it?"

"Aye."

John walked over to his horse and removed Ida Mae's carpetbag, a bedroll, and a sack. "Mum packed up some food."

"Tell her thank you. What happened last night?"

"Not too much. Most folks know us and respect us. Percy led the team. He went through the house like a wild man. Ye never did finish that fight."

"No, I never understood what it was all about. He just didn't see eye-to-eye with me since I was eight years old."

"This ain't an eight-year-old's revenge. What happened back at the mines?"

"That's what is really odd. I was actually trying to defend him when Gary Jones went after me."

"Ye were fightin' for Percy?"

"Aye. Silly, ain't it?"

John shook his head. "Keep her safe. Percy is out to destroy ye or worse. I reckon it might have to do with all the untruths he's said regarding you and the fight with Gary Jones. The

115

cabin isn't safe with Percy leading them."

"You're right. I'll plan on heading toward the next county."

"Very well. Kyle said he'd catch up with you in two days. I'll tell him to meet ye at Paw Creek."

Paw Creek was a good location. A place where, even if followed, he would appear to be going into town on business. "Tell him I'll see him there around noon."

Leather creaked as John hoisted himself up on the saddle. "Be careful, little brother. I don't like the anger I saw last night. I understand some think ye killed her and that enraged them. But when Mum and Pop said she was fine last night when she came to dinner, there were a few who believed them."

"Percy wouldn't."

"Aye, but he wasn't so bold as that. He still has to remain respectful to his uncle and aunt."

"That might not last for long."

"Aye. Keep a watchful eye. Percy might drop everything if he believes ye have moved back to Pennsylvania."

"Mayhap I should." It didn't seem fair that a man couldn't return home. But if he had stayed in Pennsylvania none of this would have happened. Olin said his good-byes to his brother, picked up his and Ida Mae's belongings, and headed back to the cave.

Orange streams of light covered the trees with a crimson layer floating above. Another hot day, he mused. Another day he wasn't married. His shoulders slumped. Why had he come home?

ও

The crack of a twig jolted Ida Mae awake. *Is someone out there?* Olin was gone. Clamping her jaw tight, she inched toward the opening. *Who is out there? Or better yet, what is out there?*

She scraped her knee on a jagged edge of rock. Keeping low, she closed the distance between herself and the opening. The dull light of dawn did little for her visibility. She craned her neck to the side and listened. Nothing! Fear swept through her. If everything were fine there would be noise of some sort.

The insects alone should be chirping away. *Shouldn't they?*

Could they have been tracked to the cave?

Ida Mae squeezed her eyes closed and prayed. *Father, help Olin and me. Help us to uncover all that has been happening in town. Reveal it to us and keep us safe. Please, Lord.*

Another twig snapped. Ida Mae willed herself closer to the ground.

"Ida Mae," Olin whispered.

Joy surged through her.

"Olin?"

"Aye, come on out. It is safe."

She ventured through the small opening and blinked. Olin stood there with his ash-stained face. "You're quite a sight."

Olin chuckled. "Ye have seen better days yourself. Come, there's a small stream where we can clean up. It has a very small swimming hole, which was fine when we were kids, but as adults I'm not sure we'll be able to submerge."

Anything was better than the ash and dirt caked on her skin. She felt like she'd rolled in mud. Of course, she probably had, sleeping in the cave. "Did you bring soap?"

"Afraid not, unless Mother packed something in the bedroll. Let me pack up our belongings and we'll get on our way." Olin slipped into the cave.

Ida Mae scanned the area. She could see the lush farmlands, small creek, and the edge of the forest. It truly was a beautiful sight.

"Shall we?" Olin pointed with her carpetbag toward the foothills of the Smoky Mountains.

Ida Mae worked her way over a small path left behind from deer and other wild animals. She didn't want to think about the other kinds of animals. She was grateful they had survived one night without noticing any unusual activities, animal or human. With each step toward the creek she realized her life was slipping away. She was on the run, hiding from some unknown stranger.

Should I stay with him? And yet the very thought of leaving him made her cringe. Would it be wiser to stay with Uncle Ty and Minnie? No, she couldn't put them at risk. Uncle Ty barely made ends meet; he didn't need anyone endangering his family or destroying his property.

Peace filled her soul when she was in Olin's arms. But that thought brought a fresh wave of heat to her cheeks. She had spent the night in Olin's arms. She should have married him. What would Minnie say? What would everyone say?

Ida Mae shook off the annoying what-ifs and continued down the path. Truth was, he was an honorable man, and they had relied on one another to keep warm in the chilly night air.

"Down here," Olin directed.

He led her around a bend to where a small, clear pool of water shimmered in the sunlight. She bent down for a drink. Her reflection in the water looked like a sickly old woman. "Ugh."

"It's not that bad." Olin bent down and unrolled the pack from his mother. "Mum sent a bar of soap." He smiled and held it up in the air.

Ida Mae jumped up to capture the sweet-smelling ball of lavender soap. She missed and jumped again. The grin on Olin's teasing face brought out the memories of her older brothers always teasing her. She faked a jump and waited for his reaction. When he swung his arm up, she tackled him. He landed on the ground with a thud. She pressed her knee into his chest and captured the soap. "Don't ever get between a woman and a bath again."

His brown eyes were as wide as saucers filled with deep rich coffee. "No, ma'am."

She offered a hand to aid him in getting up. "You do know I have two older brothers and, being the only girl in the family, I suppose I wrestled with them a bit more than if I'd had a sister."

Olin brushed off his pants. "Ye are a wonder. Ye can slip behind those rocks and make yourself ready for the bath. I'll wait around the bend. Call me when you are finished."

Her respect for Olin grew. Again, he proved himself a

gentleman and not the killer his cousin Percy claimed.

After she was bathed, and while Olin was taking his turn, she noticed something on the ridge. It appeared to be a wooden chute for gold mining. Gold mines had sprung up all over the county after gold was discovered on the Reed farm some twenty miles away. She hadn't heard of anyone striking it rich in the Charlotte area. But some farmers had found small nuggets on their land. Enough, sometimes, to help them purchase a few things they might not have without the precious ore.

"I feel better. How about you?" Olin walked up, shaking the excess water from his hair with his fingers.

Suppressing the desire to run her fingers through his silky strands, she answered, "Much."

"Ida Mae, we have a problem."

"What?"

&

Olin sat down on the rock beside her. "Ye are so beautiful."

"How is that a problem?"

How could a man convey the intensity of his desire without speaking such? *A gentleman shouldn't,* he reminded himself. He wrapped an arm around her and pulled her closer into his embrace. He brushed away a few strands of her golden hair, then captured her sweet lips. She resisted for a moment, then allowed their kiss to deepen. It took all of his strength to pull back first, closing his eyes and asking the Lord for strength. "Ida Mae. . ." His voice was huskier than he'd hoped. He cleared his throat and proceeded. "I will not dishonor thee. . . ." He let his words trail off. Her brilliant blue eyes sparkled with understanding. She turned her head.

"I should have married you."

Olin's chest swelled with—what? Pride? Desire? Or was it confidence? Yes, confidence that their love was real. Young, but very real. "Ye weren't ready."

She turned to him and placed a finger to his lips. He kissed the tip of her finger. The fresh scent of lavender mixed with her unique scent gave him renewed determination to protect this woman.

"What did John say about the visitors last night?" she asked.

"Wasn't much to say. Percy's behind it. They searched the house, found evidence that you'd been there. My parents didn't deny it. They told them the truth that ye came for dinner. They said they simply didn't know where ye were now. John also said that because my parents saw you alive and in good health several of the men didn't want to continue the search."

"Kyle gave them the impression that we might be visiting with the parson."

"If I had married you they could have honestly said we were married and having some time to ourselves for a few days."

"Sweetheart, don't fret. There will be plenty of time for marryin'. Kyle will say he's going into town in a couple days, but he'll actually be meeting us at Paw Creek at noon."

"Where do we go from here?"

To the parson, he wanted to say. "How about west and towards Kings Mountain?"

"Walkin'?"

"I could return home and pick up my horse and wagon. But I don't want to leave ye here alone in the woods."

"I can shoot."

Olin smiled and wiggled his eyebrows. "Aye, but I don't want it to be me when I return." He'd never met a woman like this one. She excited him on so many levels. She wasn't ruled by fear, and yet she had let her vulnerability show to him on more than one occasion. *Lord, please help me protect her.*

"We don't have to run. I could bring ye back to town and let the rumors die down."

"No, the sheriff wants us to hide. Someone is trying to get to me. Even if it is simply to discredit me, someone is out there. And I don't like the thought that Percy is taking advantage of it to do some damage to you as well. We have to fight this, and I think giving the sheriff a few days to sort it out is the best way."

"Mayhap." Olin sighed. Did she have to be so logical?

"There is one problem that I see from our going on the road. Will that secret matter you can't discuss with me be a problem?"

"Possibly. But it is in the Lord's hands."

"What if I go back to town without you? Then perhaps folks will think we aren't together. I can slip out in the night and return to your parents' farm."

"No, I cannot allow ye to be out on the streets by yourself. Ye must trust me."

"Olin, it isn't a matter of trust. It is a matter of deceit. Can we fool people long enough to give us an edge and a way to get to safety?"

She had a point, but everything within him shouted no. "No, ye are safe with me."

fifteen

"Where are ye going?"

"Back to your house. I'm not walking to the mountains."

Olin hustled up beside her. "And what makes ye think it is safe there?"

It's probably not. She didn't want to spend weeks on the road, in hiding, living off the land, even though she'd agreed with the sheriff the night before. Was it only last night? "Olin, I can't do this. My sensibilities are screaming this is wrong. I should stand and fight."

"Aye, and how long has your family lived in the area? Ye have a bit of the Hornet's Nest blood running through them veins."

"I reckon." Everyone knew how their ancestors had fought and held off the British during the Revolution. It was a matter of history and pride that kept the community together. Which made this misunderstanding with Olin such a puzzle. Why would the townspeople hold it against him and not believe her that he wasn't a threat?

She sat down on a fallen log along their path. Olin followed. "What's wrong?"

"If I say it doesn't make sense one more time I think I'll scream, but I have no other explanation for all of these bizarre occurrences. Why would someone steal items from my room and hide them in yours?"

"To make ye suspicious of me."

"Yes, but why?" She turned to him and reached for his hand. "Olin, I can't believe this is all about you and your past. As we said before, and the sheriff agreed, there is someone out to get me. But why?"

"Is your business a competition for another in the area?"

122

"No, and neither is yours." *So what are they after?* Ida Mae wondered. It couldn't be her wealth. There wasn't any. But some men would like the farm. "Olin, are you interested in me because of my inheritance?"

He opened his mouth in quick defense but closed it before saying a word. His eyes explored her own. A strong sense of honesty and love poured over her ruffled senses. "As we talked about before, a man could profit from your farm and the properties in town, but I am not that man. I never liked to farm. . .which bode well with my being the third son. Father has given me ten acres of land to build a house on. I do not need your farm."

A smile escaped. She knew it, but it was nice to hear it in his reassuring words once again. "But another man might."

"Perhaps. But ye professed your love to me." He wrapped her in a protective hug. "And I'm inclined to hold ye to it."

She fiddled with a loose thread on her skirt, rolling it to a ball. She silently counted to ten, willing herself not to respond to his touch. A part of her wanted to slip away and dissolve into his arms, to put an end to all the foolish thoughts that had been plaguing her since he moved into town. Another part of her wanted to stand and fight these attacks. To simply give in to Olin's protective love wouldn't accomplish a resolution to the problem. It would only forestall it.

He massaged her shoulder.

Then again, it would be so nice not to think about everything. She leaned into his chest and closed her eyes. She wasn't giving in to her emotions, she told herself, just taking a respite from circumstances.

"Father," he quietly prayed, "give us wisdom and strength. Help us find our way through this problem. Reveal to us how to expose our enemies. Guard our hearts, refine us as Ye would refine gold and silver. Thy Word says, 'The fining pot is for silver, and the furnace for gold; but the Lord trieth the hearts.' Help us to be worthy of this test."

Only a man who works with metal would equate the heart and metal, she mused. "Amen."

A surge of confidence welled up inside. "Olin, bring me home."

"But. . ."

She placed a finger to his lips. "Trust me on this. I need to return to my home, my business. I'm confident of that after your prayer."

"As ye wish. Come. . ."

They walked an hour in silence until they reached his parents' home. With each step closer, Ida Mae grew in her confidence that this is what she should do, for now. A time may come for her to go into hiding again, but for now she felt she needed to be in town, protecting her own property.

⋯

"Good morning, Mrs. Baxter, how can I help you?"

The older woman hoisted a fleece of wool onto the counter. "Been saving this for a while. I hoped to get around to it but I simply couldn't find the time. Ain't no sense letting it gather dust. What's it going to cost me?"

Ida Mae scanned the fleece. The sheep had been sheared properly. "It's not sorted."

"Nah, ain't seen much use for sorting. Them discolored parts can be sorted when you're spinning it, can't it?"

"Yes, I can sort it." *But I should charge you for sorting.* "When do you need it done by?"

"No real rush. As I said, it's been gathering dust."

Ida Mae rubbed her hand over the wool. It needed a good cleaning.

"Ain't seen nothin' like it, I tell ya."

Realizing she had missed something in the conversation, Ida Mae tried to recall Mrs. Baxter's words. Nothing came to mind. "Pardon?"

"Sheriff said it was chicken blood on your door the other day. I ain't seen nothing like that before. No good will come of it."

"Yes, very unusual." She'd been fielding questions from her customers for hours. If nothing else, the incident certainly brought in more work. "Three dollars."

"How about two?"

Ida Mae held back a chuckle. "Three. The fleece needs scoring and sorting before I can even begin to work it."

Mrs. Baxter's jowls wagged. "Oh, all right. I knew I shouldn't have left it for so long."

In reality, you should be paying me five dollars. "I'll try to have this done by the end of next week."

"That'll be just fine. Can you use some summer squash? My cupboards are overflowing."

"I'd love some." Ida Mae missed fresh vegetables.

"Bless your heart, dear." Mrs. Baxter leaned over the counter and whispered, "Have you been treated properly?"

"Yes." Again, a question that had been asked so often she'd given up being angered over it. Folks meant well, they just didn't realize the effect the question had. "I had a pleasant visit with my family and with the Orrs."

"I heard—"

"Olin Orr is a fine and decent man, in much the same way as his father and brothers. I don't understand what his cousin has against him."

The methodical nod of Mrs. Baxter's head showed she comprehended the true source of Olin's problems. "I've seen Mr. Orr's work; it's mighty fine."

A smile creased Ida Mae's cheeks. "He made me this candlestick holder."

The older woman picked it up and examined the intricate design Olin had laid out in the thin metal. The tiny tin roses at the base made the piece quite ornate. "Very nice. I might just order myself a pair."

Perhaps the blood on the doorway would be a boon to both our businesses, Ida Mae mused. "Do you want me to save the discolored wool?"

"Ain't got much use for it."

The bell over the door rang as another customer entered the shop.

"Gracious, look at the time. I must be running. I'll be in the end of next week to pick up the wool yarn." Mrs. Baxter hustled out the door with a quick greeting to Elsa Perkins.

"How can I help you, Elsa?"

"Mother's wondering if you'll have time to spin this." Elsa plopped a bundle of cotton on the counter. It was too early in the season for cotton.

"I can. What does she want?"

"Thread to sew rugs with and other thick materials."

Ida Mae scribbled a note and attached it to the bundle. "How soon would she like it?"

"Right away. Are you staying in town or going off visiting again?"

"I should be here for a while."

Elsa leaned over the counter. "Are you married?"

The sting of heat flashed across her cheeks. "No."

"I heard you had a—"

"Friend who put out a fire, nothing happened. I don't know what people are claiming they saw, but we simply spoke for a few minutes in my hallway."

"Ma said you wouldn't behave that way. I kinda figured, but it's hard when you are alone and kissin' a boy."

Ida Mae's heart went out to the young woman. "Remember, if he's a man worth marrying he'll behave proper."

"That's what I keep telling Michael." Tears trailed down Elsa's cheeks.

Ida Mae ran around the counter and swept Elsa up in her arms. "Shh, now it will be all right. Have you?"

She shook her head no.

Relief washed over Ida Mae. "Good. You tell Michael you can't see him any longer. He'll be apologizing to you right quick if he can get past your father. I suspect if you tell your parents you don't want to see Michael for a while, they'll let him know in no uncertain terms he's not welcome in your home. If he truly loves you, he'll come back and he'll be apologizing to you and your parents and be asking for your hand in marriage as a young man should. If not, he's not worth losing sleep over."

"But don't you love Olin? He's not a perfect man."

Ida Mae chuckled. "No man is a perfect man, but Olin isn't the man others say he is. I have yet to meet more of a gentleman in all of the county."

"Really? But they say—"

"Elsa, I know what they say. You can't go by what others say. You have to judge people on their actions. Olin has never put me in the same situation Michael has put you. Who do you say is more honorable?"

Elsa took in a deep breath and released it slowly. "Mr. Orr."

"Remember, a man is only as good as his words and actions. I'd say Michael has some improving to do."

"Do you really know what folks are saying about you?"

"Yes. Thankfully, I have enough people who know me and believe my word."

"Including the sheriff. He's real upset about what happened the other night. Why do you think someone poured chicken blood on your door?"

To implicate Olin.

&

"How much is this?" A constant stream of women had been in his shop all day. Eyeing him and sizing him up, no doubt.

At this very moment he'd prefer to be alone with Ida Mae in the woods, or stuck on the farm, anywhere away from these busybodies. Not one item had been purchased, but if there were a way to count fingerprints he'd have the most in a day to be certain. "Fifty cents."

"What's wrong with it? The tin man last summer tried to sell me a candlestick holder that looked very similar for two dollars."

"It's a fair price. I made the items here so I can pass on the savings to you." *And keep ye from getting overcharged by the Yankee traders.*

"Heard you married Ida Mae McAuley. Is that true? Ain't

no ring on your finger. Not that a man has to wear a ring, but my Tyrone, God bless him, always wore his wedding ring."

"No, ma'am, we are not." He'd known gossip would spread like wildfire, but he didn't anticipate it would remain, burning like coals in a firepot. For the past two days he'd been answering similar questions.

"She's a fine girl."

"Aye, that she is. Can I help you with anything else?'

The gray wisps in the woman's dark hair had him guessing her age to be around forty. The wrinkles on her hands added a few more years. Mayhap forty-five. Her features were somewhat familiar. Olin examined her a bit more closely. *Who is she?*

She picked up a snuffer and twirled it in her fingers, then placed it back on the table. "Are you truly an honorable man?"

"Pardon?"

"I've heard tales that make a person question your intent with my niece."

Olin relaxed. Seeing no one else in the shop, he closed the door and offered the customer a seat. "Mrs. Jacobs?"

"Yes."

"For you I will answer whatever ye ask. To strangers, I shall not."

Mrs. Jacobs' hands shook. "Forgive me for being direct, and I know you spoke with my husband, but for the sake of my dear departed sister's only daughter, I feel I must ask."

"I do love your niece and I hope to marry her one day. Only God knows that I've been a gentleman. There have been too many moments when we have not been in the companionship of others to vouch for my conduct. Ye may ask Ida Mae. I know the rumors circulating about the events that transpired seven years ago. Sheriff. . ."

She waved him to silence. "I am not concerned about the past, only the present. Am I correct in understanding that you spent a night alone together?"

Olin pulled at his collar. "Aye, that is the truth."

"Do you see my concern?"

"Aye, but we were trying to keep Ida Mae safe. The sheriff felt it best that Ida Mae go into hiding."

"Then why are you here now? No one has been caught."

"Ida Mae thought it best that we return. She did not want to live on the run." He still hadn't settled whether he agreed with her or not. Danger still lurked out there and he, for one, wouldn't rest until the person was apprehended.

She thought for a moment, then nodded before she spoke. "Yes, she can be that way. She's like my sister in that regard." Olin shifted as his guest scanned the room. "Do you make enough to support a wife?"

"Not at present." The words slipped out before he had a chance to think.

"Then why ask Ida Mae to marry you?"

"Because I love her and I have a savings to live on while I develop my business here."

"I see." Mrs. Jacobs narrowed her gaze. "And business is developing?"

Olin pulled at his collar once again.

"Are you planning on living off of Ida Mae's inheritance?"

"No, ma'am."

The steady drum of knocking on the closed front door made Olin grateful for the distraction. "Pardon me."

He opened the door to see Sheriff Thatcher with his arms across his chest. "Why do you keep doing this?" the sheriff asked Olin.

sixteen

The bolt clanged in the lock and relief washed over Ida Mae. Two days of nonstop customers and busybodies. The customers were all too curious and asking far too many questions for Ida Mae's liking. She leaned against the closed door and sighed. Her gaze settled on the various materials needing to be spun that were piled in a corner. The sight of it caused her back to spasm. She flipped the sign telling customers she was now closed, then pushed off the door to go to work. The constant stream of customers hadn't allowed her much time to actually spin.

She scanned the various bundles. "Where to begin?"

"With the easiest first," Minnie spouted as she came from the back room.

"How did you get. . ."

She held up a key. "You gave it to me."

Under duress. "I forgot."

"What happened here?" Minnie looked over the various piles.

"Everyone who was in the least bit curious has come by."

Minnie giggled. "Well, you won't worry about what to eat this winter. Not that you ever had to. But I'm tellin' ya, Cyrus ain't no farmer. Pa went by the place the other day and said it was a mess."

"Olin and his brothers have said the same. I know I won't be leasing the land to him next year. But I've since given up hope of seeing any profit for this year." Ida Mae sat down at the flax wheel.

"How can I help?"

"Start carding the wool or clean the cotton. Either one would be a tremendous help."

130

Minnie sat down at the counter and opened the cotton bundle from Mrs. Perkins. "Mother's in town. She might come over when she's done her shoppin'."

"Your mother hardly ever comes to town. What brought her in this time?" Ida Mae lifted some of the stringy flax fibers and rubbed them through her fingers.

"You. She's speaking with Mr. Orr right now."

"What?" The fine fibers fell to the floor.

"Don't go fussin'. She's just makin' sure Father was right about Mr. Orr."

When will this family let me make my own choices? She wanted to scream but bit her tongue to keep from exploding.

"She'll find him charmin'."

Ida Mae chuckled.

"Oh, hush now. You were right; I was wrong."

Which explained Minnie's offer to help. Her cousin could leap into anything once she had a mind to. "What about Percy?"

"What about him?"

"Weren't you and he—"

"He hasn't been around since I told him I didn't think Bobby— Olin," she corrected, "was the man he's made him out to be. I thought..." Her words trailed off.

Ida Mae knew what she thought. Minnie had hoped for a relationship with Percy, that he might be the man to spend the rest of her life with. "I'm sorry."

"Don't be. If he truly is that vengeful he'd make a horrible husband. Ain't gonna live like that. A man who can't forgive and move on with life..." Minnie shook her head. "A woman would be hard pressed to enjoy marriage with a man like that."

"Has he ever said what it was Olin did that got Percy so upset with him?"

"No."

Ida Mae wished something would come out. It didn't make sense that a cousin would hold a grudge for so long. Not when blood is thicker than water, as the saying was among the various Scots-Irish clans. Granted, Percy's father wasn't Scots-Irish, but his mother was. Ida Mae's own family tree descended from the same heritage. But her family had come to America several generations before Olin's father's, and they had long since lost their accent. Olin's accent woke something inside her. "Minnie, what if—"

"Open up, Ida Mae!" Sheriff Thatcher bellowed.

❧

Olin's heart thumped in his chest when he saw the precious blond-haired, blue-eyed maiden he'd lost his heart to. Her eyes were as big as the end of a hammer.

"Sheriff, Olin." She stepped aside to let them in.

"Miss Minnie." The sheriff lifted his hat slightly and nodded. "Your mother waits in her carriage at Mr. Orr's tin shop."

Ida Mae hugged her cousin. "Thanks."

"I'll return before we leave for home," Minnie asserted, then marched out the front door.

Olin held back a laugh, thankful he wasn't called to be Minnie Jacobs's spouse. He worked his way around the sheriff and sidled up beside Ida Mae, capturing her in a protective embrace. "The sheriff has some interesting news."

"Miss McAuley, are you aware that Percy Mandrake has been arrested?"

Ida Mae relaxed in Olin's arms. He gave her a gentle squeeze, encouraged that his cousin no longer posed a threat to him or, more importantly, to Ida Mae.

"Why?"

"Drunk and disorderly."

"He claims he was responsible for putting the chicken blood on the entrance," Olin supplied. She needed to know that the threat was gone.

"Did he admit to anything else?"

"No, ma'am, only the blood."

"Why?"

"He didn't say. He succumbed to the liquor and fell asleep."

"Does this mean I'm safe?"

"I'd wager to say it is a safe bet. Percy's been after Olin since he came back to town. He even came to my office to report Olin's past crimes."

"So all of this was about you and not me?"

Olin turned and faced her. "This is where the sheriff and I disagree. The notes were personal to you. Sheriff feels—"

"I can speak for myself," Sheriff Thatcher chided Olin. "The first note said to get rid of your tenant, that would be Olin, and we know how Percy felt about him. The second note revealed someone had been watching your place in the middle of the night. Again, it was an indirect reference to Olin."

"But what about the stolen items?"

"They were hidden in Olin's area of the shop."

Olin had to admit it made sense, but something in the pit of his gut told him there was something else going on here. Someone else was still after Ida Mae, but he couldn't understand who or why.

"So, I am safe." Ida Mae breathed a sigh of relief.

Olin's spine stiffened. A tiny muscle in his jaw started to twitch.

"Thank you, Sheriff Thatcher, for all your hard work on my behalf."

"Just doin' my job, Ida Mae. Olin, don't forget that special project. The customer is hoping to get a look at the design next week."

"Tell him it will be ready."

Ida Mae furrowed her brows. Olin reached for his collar and pulled. How long could he keep this a secret? If she were his wife, it wouldn't be a problem. His mind spun off in various directions. It's not that he didn't want to share the information with Ida Mae. Actually, he was longing to tell her. But the reality was, if he didn't keep the secret it would affect Mr. Bechtler and his plans to make the first gold coin in the area. A mint near the mines seemed like a brilliant plan. Presently, the gold was shipped up to Washington to be minted there. As much as he wanted to tell Ida Mae, he couldn't.

"Sheriff Thatcher"—Ida Mae turned her attention from Olin

back to the sheriff—"am I really safe now?"

"It appears that way. I'd like you to continue to be cautious. Also, be aware that everyone in town is watching you now."

And me. Olin's mind drifted back over his day and the many curiosity seekers. "We'll be careful."

The sheriff paused for a moment, then gave a lift of his hat and departed.

"How was your day?" Olin asked before stepping aside and giving Ida Mae some room.

"Busy. And yours? I heard my aunt came by to see you."

Olin smiled. "She needed her heart settled—like your uncle."

"Do you think Percy was our problem?"

"If the sheriff believes that to be the case, I guess I do, too, although I'm still uncomfortable. Mayhap it could be we've lived in fear for so long our minds need time to adjust."

"Will you be moving back into the shop?"

I'd love to. "No. For now I believe I should stay where I am. Are ye hungry?"

"Starving."

"Mum came into town to invite you to dinner."

"Olin, tell your mother thank you, but I have to spend most of the night working. I need to get caught up on this rash of orders. I know most of them are from folks who didn't really need the work done, but some are legitimate requests. All these little orders will stop me from completing the bigger orders."

"Aye, I understand. I'll be working late tonight as well." He didn't want to tell her the gossip was so bad that when he closed his shop door with Ida Mae's aunt inside someone had gone running to the sheriff to report his illicit behavior. "I miss you."

She turned in his embrace and nuzzled her head under his chin. "I've missed you, too."

He kissed the top of her head. "I better go back to my shop or my parents will wonder what happened to me."

She stepped out of his embrace, and the cool wind of separation washed over him. He wanted her in his arms.

Olin dropped them to his sides. *I can't give in to my emotions. Not now.*

"I'll see you tomorrow." The gentle whoosh of her skirt followed her back to the spinning wheel.

Olin stepped out the front door. "Don't forget to lock it." The bright setting sun caused him to blink. Could their troubles be truly over? Was Percy responsible for everything? And why the blood?

ᕀ

Ida Mae worked until midnight. She finished a large order and several of the smaller ones. Tomorrow she'd work on John Alexander's newest order. He had pressed to have this one filled as soon as possible. She supposed it had something to do with the amount of people who had come through her door the previous two days.

Before bed she swept the floors and checked the locks. A twinge of hunger rumbled in her stomach, reminding her she hadn't eaten since breakfast. In the back room she cut a slice of bread, sliced a tomato, and sprinkled it with basil, salt, and pepper. She then peeled the layer of wax off a small ball of cheese she had made last week.

A flash of a memory of being in Olin's arms wiggled past her tired senses. *Lord, how can I love him so much having known him for so little time? Do I truly love him or am I caught up in the emotions and fear because of the events that have happened?*

Memories of the day's conversations swam through her mind as she sat down to eat her makeshift dinner. It bothered her that so many people had come just to satisfy their curiosity. And yet it was typical for the area. Many genuinely cared what happened to her, others were just busybodies trying to get the next tidbit they could share with someone else.

Ida Mae bit into the soft ball of cheese, a delicacy her mother had taught her to make. It melted well and was great for heating over a slice of toast. She'd love an open toasted cheese sandwich with tomato and basil right now, but her meal, such as it was, would have to do.

Closing her eyes, Ida Mae sat and enjoyed the peaceful night sounds. A distant owl hooted. Night insects hummed, building in intensity as the rest of the world's silence deepened. "If only life could remain this calm."

Taking in a deep sigh, she quickly finished her meal, cleaned up, and went to bed. Morning would be sneaking up on her if she didn't get to sleep soon. As she snuggled into her pillow, thoughts of Olin and being in his arms drifted back. "Lord, I should have married him. But—I'm doing it again, always questioning, never going with my first instinct. Why? Why can't I just make a decision and stick with it? Why do I flounder so?

"On the other hand, Father isn't around to give his blessing to Olin. I haven't known him all that long, and is physical attraction enough? How can a girl court when her parents are gone? How does one know if she is making the right choice?

"Then again, others seem to marry quickly and enjoy a happy marriage. Is a long courtship necessary to know if this person is to be your spouse?"

Ida Mae tossed and turned for thirty minutes, pondering these questions before falling asleep. She awoke the next morning with the same questions buzzing around in her head.

She dressed and made a large breakfast for herself, one that would hold a farmer all day if necessary, and she expected to have a similar day today as she had the day before. After breakfast she cleaned up and went out the back door to throw the dirty water away.

Fear spiraled down her legs like the wool circling the large spinner's wheel, tying her in place.

seventeen

Olin dug his spurs into the horse's side to catch up to the swarm of people huddled around Ida Mae's back door. He'd hoped to have a few minutes alone with her before they started their day. He jumped off the horse. Worming his way through the crowd, he called out, "Ida Mae?"

She stood there frozen, with tears running down her cheeks. He came up beside her. "Ida Mae."

"Get your hands off of her."

"Pardon?" Olin turned to see a man holding a knife.

"You heard me. Miss McAuley didn't have any problems until you moved into town."

"Stop!" Ida Mae cried and reached out toward Olin. "Cyrus, Olin is my friend."

"Ida Mae, you've gotta see that he's the cause of all your problems."

"No. He isn't. You're the one who scared me this morning."

A surge of anger pulsed through Olin. He opened and closed his fists. He had little patience for Cyrus Morgan, who had a wife but let rumors continue that Ida Mae was his wife. A man who claimed to be a farmer but turned her farm into a dirt farm where even weeds wouldn't grow. What was he doing with an unsheathed knife? "Folks, you can go about your business. I'll—good morning, Sheriff."

Sheriff Thatcher made his way to the center of the crowd. "What seems to be the problem?"

"Cyrus Morgan startled me this morning. He came to deliver a ham but all I saw was his large knife when I opened the door."

"I see." The sheriff turned toward Cyrus. "Is this true?"

"Yes, sir." Cyrus lifted the smallest smoked ham Olin had

ever seen. He truly was a miserable farmer. "I came to deliver this from the farm."

"Mr. Orr, what brings you here this morning?"

"I came to check on Miss McAuley before opening my shop."

The sheriff nodded, then turned back to the crowd. "Y'all can go on now. I've got the matter in hand." Then he turned toward Ida Mae. "Are you all right?"

She nodded.

"Mr. Morgan, why don't you give me the ham? Mr. Orr, why don't you head on to your place of business?"

Olin stared in disbelief. Did the sheriff now consider him a suspect? Sheriff Thatcher winked.

Olin fought the desire to stay planted and ask a million questions. Instead, he abided with the sheriff's wishes and mounted his horse. He could hear Cyrus do the same behind him. He didn't want to leave Ida Mae, but he saw something in the sheriff's eyes, something akin to a gentle sternness that said, "Let me do my job."

Olin would let him for the time being. But the first opportunity he had he'd be at Ida Mae's door. He didn't like the look of Cyrus's knife, and could well imagine the fear it had caused her. "Lord, please keep her safe."

Olin arrived at his shop, dismounted, and readied his horse for the stable. *I should go back.* He tossed the saddle on the rail of the stall. *But the sheriff said to come here. Why?* He reached for the oats and filled the bin. "This is nonsense. I should be with her. I should be protecting her."

He grabbed the water bucket to top off the trough. After a couple of stiff cranks, the pump poured water into the bucket. "But Percy is locked up, isn't he? So where is the threat?"

❧

Ida Mae held on to the banister just a few minutes longer, hoping that her legs were no longer rubber. "What's the matter, Sheriff?"

"You tell me. I come into work this morning and there's a

crowd gathering at your home. Doesn't make a man content with all that's been happening."

"It's as I said, I saw the knife and couldn't move. I'm afraid I can't tell you who gathered or when they gathered. It's all a blank to me. The only thing I remember is Olin calling my name."

"I see. Did Cyrus actually come to bring you a ham?"

"Apparently. It's my portion of the pig he slaughtered last week."

"Wasn't very big."

"No, I can see that." Ida Mae released the railing. "Would you like to come inside?"

"No, I think we've given the neighbors quite enough to talk about today."

Absolutely. "I'm fine, Sheriff."

Sheriff Thatcher nodded with the tip of his hat. "I'll be off. I'll come around and check on you at noon."

"Thank you."

Ida Mae went into her room and collapsed on her bed. How could she have overreacted so? She'd seen large knives many times. Just about every man carried one in some form or fashion. But still, it was odd to see such a huge knife to simply cut the string he was using to hold the ham up on a nail.

Why would the sheriff send Olin away? "Time to face the day."

Several hours later, Olin returned. Together they discussed her tired nerves and his desire to take her away from all of this. Her love for Olin deepened as she watched him be more concerned about her and her interests than his own.

The next few days passed without incident. Even the constant stream of customers had slowed down to an occasional one or two a day. All caught up on her work, Ida Mae made a picnic lunch to bring to Olin. Today they would finally have some time alone, she hoped. They'd had dinner with his parents one night, but Kyle had escorted her back to the town. Time alone was at an all-time premium. If it wasn't the sheriff constantly separating them for some unknown reason, it was his family. *Do they not want me to marry Olin?* Ida Mae's step faltered at the thought.

She had sent a note to Olin earlier in the day to let him know her intentions. The door to his shop was closed. *Odd.*

Olin leaned against the stable doorway. "Hello."

She turned to the left. "Hello" His handsome face glowed. Ida Mae's heart clenched. She did love this man. A few days of calm allowed her to trust her instincts and not question whether she loved him only because he'd come to her rescue on more than one occasion.

❧

Ida Mae quickened her pace and came up beside him. "I've been looking forward to this for days."

Olin chuckled. "You only sent me an invitation this morning. Where are we going?"

"There's a spot on the river at my farm." *That's quite romantic*, she didn't add.

His smile slipped. "Honey, I can't be gone that long. I have orders to finish."

Ida Mae took a moment to inhale deeply and exhale slowly. She suspected that might be the case but had hoped he could simply close his doors the way she had. "I understand. But a girl can hope."

"Why don't we plan on going there after church on Sunday?"

"There's another church picnic."

"Ah, all right. How about—"

"Let's just go to the edge of town on the green overlooking the northeast corner," she suggested.

"Fine, you ride. I'll escort ye."

Ida Mae mounted and sat sidesaddle. "Olin, are your parents not—"

"No. They had Kyle bring ye to town for your honor. They felt ye have had enough trouble, so if someone other than me escorted ye home, they thought it wouldn't produce as much gossip."

"Probably so. But I prefer your company."

"And I prefer yours. Ye are the sweetest joy in my life."

They traveled a few blocks to the edge of the town and sat down on the green knoll overlooking the Wingate plantation. Slaves worked in the distant fields. It seemed odd to see so many. Most, if not all, of the yeoman farmers didn't own slaves. Olin reclined and leaned on his elbow. " 'Tis a fine day, lass."

"Yes."

"Now that we be alone, tell me what happened the other day with Cyrus."

"It's as he said, he came to deliver the ham and I froze at seeing that huge knife when I opened the door. I'm certain it was an overreaction due to the events that have transpired."

"Aye, ye are probably right. That was a right small ham."

Ida Mae giggled. "Tender, though. But yes, I think he killed one of the young ones. Perhaps they were low on food."

"Honey, ye should consider hiring Kyle to look after your farm."

"Trust me, I have been. I've written to my brothers and warned them that we'll receive little, if any, income this year. I've heard back from Bryan and he said not to fret over it. All indications are he'll be having a bumper crop this year. He also suggested that I sell the property and come live with him and his wife."

Olin stiffened.

It pleased Ida Mae to see that reaction in him. He truly did care about her.

"Selling your farm is an answer, but it's good land and should make ye a profit if it is farmed well."

She couldn't agree with him more. But she didn't want to spend the entire hour speaking about such matters. "Olin, I've missed you."

He sat up and slid closer. "Aye."

"Why did the sheriff tell you to leave the other day?" Sheriff Thatcher hadn't said a word about it to her, and she knew it had to do with appearances. But really, it was daylight, and they were in public. Who should be concerned about her and Olin speaking with one another?

"I'm not certain. Mayhap he suspects someone else besides Percy."

"Do you think I'm still in danger?"

"I don't know. But nothing has happened since Percy was arrested."

"True." Ida Mae pondered her own fears and concerns. "I haven't seen any sign of anyone breaking in or attempting to. There have been no notes—"

Olin jumped up. "That's what has been bothering me about this. I hadn't been able to put my finger on it, but that's it." Olin paced back and forth on the knoll.

"Finger on what?"

"The notes. Percy couldn't have written those. He might have had someone help him, but he didn't stay in school past third grade. He's been working on the farm all his life. He doesn't read well. And he certainly can't construct the penmanship we saw on those notes."

Prickly brushes of gooseflesh rose on her body. Someone was still out there who wanted to do harm to her. "Then who?"

"I don't know. But I'll not have ye spend another night in that building."

"But—"

Olin laid a finger to her lips. "I think we should put ye in hiding for a day or two and see what happens. The old cottage on my parents' place is clean and ready. I'll sneak out there tonight and bring food and supplies."

"No. I can't go on the run again."

"But ye must. Don't ye see, we have to bring whoever is after ye out of the woodwork. I won't go with ye. I'll come to work and pretend to be shocked and see what interest that brings."

"But the sheriff. . ."

"Will question me as long as the day has light, plus some, I'm afraid. I'll be his prime suspect."

"Shouldn't we tell him?"

"Mayhap, but let's pray about this. I don't want us running off without the Lord's blessing."

Ida Mae didn't want that, either. She didn't want to be running off, period. She certainly didn't want to go in hiding in a cottage with no one around, alone, and without visitors, without Olin. Her body ached to be held in his arms.

⁂

Olin silently prayed he was doing what the Lord would have him do. Something about Cyrus Morgan still bothered him. And he still didn't have a clear picture as to why the sheriff would have him leave Ida Mae's side after a horrific experience. He didn't want to believe the sheriff was aware or possibly involved with the strange events. It couldn't be that, he argued with himself for the twentieth time since the incident. After having some measure of peace about hiding Ida Mae in the cabin, he left her on the knoll. She rode off to his house, never returning to her business.

He went back to work as if nothing had happened. It wasn't long before Sheriff Thatcher came knocking at his door. "Olin."

"Sheriff."

"Where is she?"

Who? he wanted to ask but decided not to bait the sheriff. "In hiding."

"What's happened?"

"Nothing."

The sheriff rubbed the back of his neck. "Then why? And I want more than a single word or two response, understand?"

"Percy couldn't have written those notes. His skills are limited in those areas. He only finished third grade. After that he worked on the farm."

"I thought education was a major part of your kin's heritage."

"Aye, but Percy's father is not Scots-Irish. He doesn't see education to be as important as his mother's family does."

The sheriff leaned back on the edge of the counter. "Then you went back to my original plan to hide her to flush out the culprits."

"More or less. This time I'm not hiding. This should rattle

whoever is after her. If I'm in the dark as to where she is, then he truly will be."

"You'll be watched."

"I suspect so. I'll join her in a few days if nothing develops." Olin reached for his tin snips and cut the edge off the piece he had been working on when the sheriff came in.

"You two have kept my hands full the past few months."

"Aye, I'm truly sorry for that. But I think this goes beyond Percy and his hatred toward me."

"I believe you are probably right. I've heard some rumblings lately that suggest someone might be trying to persuade Ida Mae to marry him so he can have her property."

"Who?"

Sheriff guffawed. "Half the folks say it's you."

Olin dropped the snips.

"Hang on, son. I didn't say I believed them. I believe there is some truth in this rumor, along with others. Ida Mae in hiding might just bring some to the surface. You have to trust me. I can't tell you who I suspect because of that temper of yours."

"What temper? I haven't done—"

"*That* temper. You control it, yes, but it still flares. I saw it the other morning, too. Can you trust me?"

"Do you trust me?" Olin wasn't sure he wanted to hear the answer.

"Yes."

Olin's shoulders relaxed. "All right, I'll trust ye."

"Good. When you see Ida Mae, pass on a message to her. Let her know I'm aware and am still investigating."

"Yes, sir."

Olin watched the sheriff leave and went back to work. The minutes ticked by at the speed of a snail crossing the street. He couldn't go to her tonight. He'd have to send John or Kyle to go to town and then sneak around to the cottage. Whoever the sheriff was after would certainly be watching. He fought the desire to go to Ida Mae's side. He wanted to protect her but his best protection was to stay away. *Lord, help her understand.*

eighteen

For two days Ida Mae prayed, read, and reread the scriptures, partly out of boredom, but also because she was searching for answers. Not that anyone could ever truly understand the ways of God. Perhaps she should sell the property and move in with her brother Bryan and his wife. If it weren't for the properties she owned in town, the little income she made from spinning would not support her.

And where was Olin, and how did he fit in this conflict? Every time they tried to spend a moment with one another something came up. It reminded her of the corduroy roads in the area—up, down, up, down, bumpy at best.

The passage from Proverbs that she and Olin had shared the first time she went on the run repeatedly came back to mind. But after two days with no human contact, Ida Mae felt like screaming. She settled for a cool bath in the creek, the same stream she had bathed in the day she was supposed to marry Olin. That day seemed like an eternity ago.

She wouldn't stay here much longer. Instead, she figured, she should travel to her brother's home in Kentucky and visit with them for the winter if nothing changed. Dressed and ready to take her bath, she slipped out of the cabin and headed for the stream. She figured it would take a forty-five-minute walk, if she had her bearings straight. Generally, she was pretty good with directions, but her current ability to concentrate was sorely diminished.

A horse and rider approached, and it was too late to hide. Ida Mae continued her walk, then noticed it was Olin's mother.

"Ida Mae!" Mrs. Orr called out. "How are ye?"

Relieved. "Fine, I was going to take a bath."

"Let me join you."

Company sounded good. Mrs. Orr slipped off her horse and walked beside her. "How are ye really?"

"Bored."

Mrs. Orr chuckled. "Aye, I would be, too. Can I bring ye some more books?"

Ida Mae nodded. She always loved to read, although at this moment in time she wished for something else. "Do you have a spinning wheel?"

"Aye. Would ye like some cotton to spin? I finished the wool."

"That would be wonderful." *Anything would be wonderful, even weaving.* Ida Mae mentally ducked as she imagined her mother listening from heaven at that thought.

"Do ye need more food?"

"Not yet."

"I don't understand why ye can't stay in the big house with us. Olin says ye need to be in hidin', and I suppose he knows, but it seems silly. We don't get many visitors here."

"That would be nice." As bored as she was, it was more comfortable than having to be social, especially in her dark moods of regret and wondering why things had gone so wrong in her life since her parents died.

"I came to tell ye that Percy is out of jail. The judge told him to pay restitution for the damages and he was free to go."

"Percy knows about the cabin."

"Aye."

"Am I safe?"

Mrs. Orr grabbed her hand and squeezed it. "I don't know, lass."

❧

Olin walked into the sheriff's office as ordered. "Sheriff."

"Mr. Orr, take a seat. I'll be right with you."

Amos Bentley stood a few feet from the sheriff. "I'm tellin' ya, Sheriff, it's those miners. I'm losing livestock left and right. Ain't like they can't afford to pay for their food."

"I'll look into it."

Amos nodded. "I'll check in next week."

"You do that, Amos. Have a good day." The sheriff stepped toward his desk, sat down, and wrote a note. Then he raised his head to focus on Olin. "We've got a problem."

"What?"

"Someone broke into Ida Mae's room. They tore it apart and. . ." The sheriff seemed to be collecting his thoughts. "And left evidence that she struggled and was possibly killed."

"What? Who?"

"I don't know. She's safe, right?"

"Aye. I've watched from a distance, but I can tell she's still at the cabin."

"Good. 'Cause there are more problems."

Olin braced himself.

"I hate to do this, son, but it appears you were the one to kidnap her."

"Pardon?" Olin held on to the arms of the oak chair so tightly his hands started to shake.

"Exactly. You're being framed for Ida Mae's murder."

"By whom?"

"If I knew that we wouldn't be having this conversation."

"What do we do now?"

"We wait. It's early and most folks aren't aware yet that something has happened. As you know, news travels fast in these parts and I expect to find folks in an uproar. Would you mind spending the day behind bars?"

"That doesn't make sense."

"I know. But I suspect you'll be framed for some other crime that I can't disprove and you'll end up behind bars anyway. If you are already in jail that won't be possible."

"But. . ." Olin clamped his mouth shut. Anything he said right now was being weighed. There seemed to be some level of doubt in the sheriff's eyes. *At the moment he seems to believe me.*

"Olin. . ." The sheriff's words trailed off as the door banged open.

Cyrus Morgan bustled in with the weight of a sledgehammer. "Sheriff, I. . ." He paused and focused on Olin, then narrowed his gaze. "Ida Mae is missing."

"I'm aware of that."

Cyrus finally broke his gaze and looked at the sheriff. "What are you doing about it?"

"I'm looking into the matter. She might be visiting—"

"Her room has been ransacked."

The sheriff leaned back. "And you know this how?"

Cyrus stammered. "A—a friend told me."

"Care to name names?"

Cyrus stepped back. "Rosey Turner."

Rosey Morgan, your wife, Olin wanted to blurt out.

"And how did Rosey hear this?"

Cyrus stretched his neck to the side. "I don't know. She just told me and I came running over here. Ida Mae and Rosey's family are good friends. As you know, I rebuilt her house and am running her farm this year."

"Yes." The sheriff relaxed his posture. "I appreciate your concerns, Mr. Morgan. But, as you see, I already knew and am investigating it fully."

Cyrus's gaze shifted back to Olin, then to Sheriff Thatcher. "Let me know if you find out anything. Ida Mae and I were close." He pulled a paper from his pocket and handed it to the sheriff. "Real close. And if you ask me, I think Mr. Orr has some questions to answer. She probably refused his advances—"

"Mr. Orr, sit down!" the sheriff bellowed as Olin shot to his feet. "And why was this a secret?" The sheriff held up the piece of paper.

What could be on it? Olin tried to get a glance but couldn't. It looked to be a parchment of some sort, fairly new but very wrinkled.

"Ida Mae asked me to keep our marriage a secret."

"Marriage?" Olin squeaked as he dropped back into his chair.

"Yes, she and I married a few months back." Cyrus grinned.

How can that be? Olin gripped the arms of the chair. *Father, give me grace and strength.*

"Cyrus, this does put an interesting spin on my investigation. If this paper is real—and I will be checking into its validity—then I will need to check Ida Mae's farmhouse to see that she's not at home with you."

"Of course she's not at home. Why would I come here to you if she were at home?"

"I don't know. Why would you keep the marriage a secret?"

Olin found his voice. "I heard rumors that Cyrus married Ida Mae several months back."

Cyrus grinned. "I got drunk one night and let it slip out. But ever since I've kept my mouth shut. Ida Mae wanted to keep it a secret—something to do with the settlement of her parents' estate. I told her I didn't care about the inheritance. She had to work things out with her brothers, though. They wanted to sell the properties, but Ida Mae and I wanted to keep the farm."

"I see." The sheriff shifted back in his seat and scanned the document in front of him. "Who's the judge?"

"Judge Weaver from Montgomery County."

The sheriff simply nodded.

"Ida Mae felt it would help keep our secret longer. Ya know how folks can be around here."

Olin didn't know what to believe. How could she have married this man? It didn't fit. *And why would she proclaim her love for me and attempt to marry me but not go through with it?* Dread washed over him. Is this why she couldn't, because she was already married to Cyrus? Olin's anger shifted from Cyrus to Ida Mae.

"Pardon me. You two obviously have a lot to discuss. I hope ye find your wife, Mr. Morgan." Olin slipped out of the sheriff's office. The bright sun caused him to close his eyes. *How could I have been such a fool?*

❧

"Ida Mae, are ye through, lass?" Mrs. Orr called out from behind the bush.

Leaning her head back under the cool water, Ida Mae rinsed her hair again. "I'll be right there." Summer bathing in the river was such a delight. It was far less work, and the gentle roll of a stream seemed to relax one's muscles, rather than having to fill your own tub and drain it after you were cleaned.

On shore, Ida Mae dried herself off.

"Are ye decent?"

"More or less." She wouldn't want to be caught in her underclothing with anyone else but felt comfortable enough with Mrs. Orr.

"Would ye like me to brush out your hair?"

Memories of childhood flooded back in her mind, of sitting in front of her mother and father and having them brush her golden strands. "That would be wonderful, thank you."

"You're welcome. Here, sit down on this rock.

"I haven't been able to do this for years. I'd come down to the river with the girls and we'd bathe and brush one another's hair. It was a grand time. It's much more peaceful this morning than the last time ye and I were down here."

The wedding day. Her stomach flipped, then flopped like a spindle too heavy with thread. "I think I should have gone through with the wedding." Ida Mae felt the heat rise in her cheeks.

Mrs. Orr's hands stilled. "Don't regret saying no, child. If ye weren't ready it is not a good thing to start a marriage with doubt."

"I know, but it might have made life simpler. You wouldn't believe the people who have come to me because of the gossip they've heard. If I had run off and married Olin, then no one would say anything."

"Oh, I think they'd be inclined to still say a few words. But ye are probably right that they would have had less to say."

"Can I ask you something?" Ida Mae spun around and faced Mrs. Orr.

"I'd be honored."

How could she word this? "Do you think it is wise for me to go into hiding? I mean, shouldn't I be facing my problems and not running away from them?"

Mrs. Orr took a moment, then sat down beside Ida Mae. "From what Olin Robert has told me, ye are hiding because for some unknown reason someone may want to hurt you."

"That's one rumor. The other is that someone is out to discredit Olin. Percy, for example."

"Aye, Percy has never been a content man. He's always wanted more out of life than what he was willing to work for. And he has a mean streak that runs deep in his heart, though one rarely sees it. Generally, Percy is a good and kind man. But with Olin—well, those two never saw eye-to-eye on anything."

"But why would Percy want Olin out of the area?"

"Probably because he fears that folks would learn that Bobby was protecting him from Gary Jones."

What? "I thought it was just the two of them that got into a fight. How was Percy involved?"

"From what I can piece together, and mind ye, my boy won't tell me straight what happened that day, Percy must have done something or owed Jones some money, and he was wanting restitution. Olin tried to distract him so that he wouldn't take his rage out on Percy. Angry words built to fisticuffs. There were a few of the older men on the crew who told Mr. Orr and myself bits and pieces of what happened. Over time, Percy seems to have forgotten that he was the true cause for the fight. Truth is, Olin won't speak of the matter. He feels so guilty for killing a man, and he's taken full responsibility for the incident. As well he should. No matter what Percy may or may not have done, it was Olin who fought the man and it was his fist that actually killed him. He's always had a temper, and it got the best of him that day."

Ida Mae started to shake. If she married Olin would he get so angry with her that he might...

"Now, child, I can see it in your eyes ye are afraid of him. I'm so sorry. What ye may not know is that when we sent him to Pennsylvania he was mentored by a man who had a similar problem with his temper. Oh, he never killed a man, but he came close. Anyway, his mentor showed him how to curb his anger, give it over to the Lord, and remain in control. I truly believe Olin has changed. Look at all that has happened to you. Olin Robert has not lifted an angry hand to anyone and he's remained calm. Oh, I've seen the anger spark for a moment or two, but he's controlling it. 'Tis a sweet answer to prayer."

Ida Mae relaxed. She'd seen it, too. "So you think Percy is out to discredit Olin because he fears Olin will tell everyone what really happened?"

"Aye, and I believe money was involved, too, but I haven't been able to figure if that is the case or not."

Olin, we need to talk. There can't be any secrets between us.

nineteen

Olin hustled from the sheriff's office to Ida Mae's. Instantly his nostrils filled with the coppery scent of blood. Her bedding was pulled in different directions, giving the appearance of a struggle. A dark brown trail of blood angled off the bottom sheet. Fear washed over him. Had Ida Mae returned from the cottage? Had something happened to her?

He bolted from her room and ran to the stable where he kept his horse. Saddled, he hopped on and headed home. A chill ran down his spine. *What if someone is watching?* He pulled the reins. The horse halted.

He sat there for ten minutes, not sure what to do next. He should check on Ida Mae, but then again, the sheriff said there had been evidence suggesting he might have been the one who broke into Ida Mae's. He thought back on the scene in her room. Had it been staged? Had someone come in and planned that chaos?

If they had, they would have been watching him. And probably had been for the past two days since Ida Mae went into hiding. *No, I can't check on her. Mayhap after nightfall.*

He urged the horse forward and continued toward the house. He could send someone to check on Ida Mae. He would still need to talk with her, but it was imperative that he knew for certain that she was still in the cottage and safe.

Married? How could that be? She didn't speak favorably of Cyrus and planned not to let him farm the land next year. If he were her husband, could she do that? Wouldn't she try to help him learn how to farm? *She can't be married, Lord, she just can't be. She's not the kind to be double minded.*

His mind whirled with questions. The Ida Mae he knew would never attach herself to someone like Cyrus Morgan. But how much did he know about her, really? Memories flooded his thoughts of their few intimate times alone, of the kisses they shared.

"Lord, please help me understand. Am I a fool?"

There was something about Cyrus he never cared for. Was it that he saw a hidden relationship between him and Ida Mae? She had said he had asked her to marry him on more than one occasion. Had it gone further? Was she really married? But if they were, why wasn't Cyrus helping her run from her troubles, putting her in hiding?

The weight in his chest plummeted to his gut. "Lord, give me strength."

❧

Under the cloak of darkness, Olin headed out to the cottage. He'd been relieved to hear from his mother that Ida Mae was well. He didn't tell his family about Ida Mae's marriage to Cyrus Morgan. He wanted to hear from her first. He'd been in an awful mood since coming home. He spent the day cleaning the stalls, chopping wood, anything to keep his body busy and wear off some of the tension and anger he felt.

He'd know in a few short minutes her side of the story.

A dim light burned in the window.

"Ida Mae!" he called before he got off his horse. "It's Olin."

The front door creaked open. "Has something happened?"

That's an understatement. Calm down, calm down. Let her explain what happened. "Yes. Someone broke into your room and made it look like there was a struggle and left some blood behind."

Ida Mae wobbled.

Olin reached her in a couple quick steps. "Can I come in?"

She nodded.

Lord, give me the grace. Help me give her reasonable doubt.

They sat down. Her hands trembled in her lap.

Silently, he let out a long, deep breath. "Ida Mae, there isn't an easy way to address this. Cyrus Morgan heard of the break-in and gave the sheriff. . ." He paused and rubbed the back of his neck. *She couldn't have, could she?* "He gave the sheriff his marriage license."

She lifted her head and knitted her eyebrows. "He finally told folks?"

"Aye."

Ida Mae sighed. "Good. I didn't want to keep that secret any longer."

"So it's true?"

"Yes."

Olin jumped up from his seat and began to pace. *How could she have fooled me so?* The drumming of his pulse echoed in his ears. "Why?"

"Why what?"

"Why did ye marry him?"

"Marry him? What are you talking about, Olin?"

❦

Ida Mae couldn't understand the mood Olin was in. If the floor were flint and he were steel, the cottage would have exploded by now. "Olin, talk to me. What are you talking about? I didn't marry anyone."

"Cyrus says ye and he were married in Montgomery County several months back."

"He said what? He married Rosey Turner, not me." So Cyrus was behind all the rumors. "Why would he say such a thing?"

"Ye swear ye aren't married to Cyrus?"

"Olin, how could you think such a thing? I nearly married you a few weeks ago. Would I do that if I were married to another man?"

Olin collapsed in the seat. Ida Mae went on her knees in front of him. Reaching for his hands, she held them. *He has to know the truth.* "I love you, Olin. I never loved or ever had a desire to marry Cyrus. Oh, I gave it a fleeting thought once, but it did not stay with me for more than a few hours. Of course, that's when I found out he married Rosey Turner."

He rubbed the top of her hands with his thumbs. "He has a certificate, Ida Mae. Sheriff read it."

"And it has my name on it?"

"Apparently. Thatcher didn't let me see it."

"I don't understand how he could have gotten my signature. It has to be a forgery."

"The sheriff's trying to verify your signature. I hadn't thought of that."

Doubt filled her. If Olin truly loved her, would he have believed the words of Cyrus Morgan? "You don't believe me, do you?"

"I'm trying. I can't understand how he'd have a marriage certificate with your name on it, if you weren't there. It looked like a legal document to me."

"Legal document?" Ida Mae's mind flickered back to the time when Cyrus came in to sign paperwork for the rental agreement to the farm. Her eyes widened. "Oh no."

"What?"

"I signed papers for our rental agreement, just as you and I did. Do you suppose he slipped another paper in there and had me sign it? That can't be legal, can it? I can't be married to him, can I? And what would Rosey say? She told me they had gotten married."

Ida Mae released his hands, got up, and started to pace, just as he had done a few moments before.

"There be more."

She froze mid-stride. Icicles crystallized down her spine. *What else could go wrong, Lord?*

"The sheriff said there was evidence that made me look like the intruder."

Ida Mae relaxed. "At least he knew where I was and that you didn't have anything to do with it."

"Aye, that be a blessin'," he acknowledged. "Ida Mae, I hate to say this, but do you think Cyrus could be the one who's been causing the problems?"

She shook her head no, then realized everything started when she discovered he had married Rosey. Of course, that was nearly the same day Olin moved into town. "Is he behind it all, or did Percy have a part to play in that?" She sat back down. Now was the time for them to get to the bottom of all their problems, and this included Olin's past. "Your mother told me that Percy had something to do with you getting in that fight years ago."

"Don't—" A knock at the door stopped their conversation.

twenty

Olin didn't know whether or not to be grateful for the interruption. The story of the past was long dead and buried and he wanted to keep it that way. What he didn't expect to see on the other side of the door was Sheriff Thatcher. "Evenin', Olin."

"Evenin'. What brought ye out here this time of night?"

Ida Mae came up and stood behind him, slipping her hand into his.

"I'm just returning from Montgomery County. The justice of the peace there has a record of Cyrus Morgan marrying Ida Mae on June third of this year."

"It can't be. I never married him, I swear."

The sheriff tipped back his hat. "That's what I expected you to say. So I asked the JP to come by my office tomorrow morning around ten A.M. I'd like you, Ida Mae, to arrive ten minutes later. Cyrus will be there already. My goal is to catch Cyrus in his lie."

"Cyrus is behind all of this?"

"Not all of it. As best I can figure, there were one or two incidents when Percy was involved. I'll deal with him later. What concerns me now is Cyrus, and I'm afraid his plans for Ida Mae may not be healthy."

Olin's back went ramrod straight. Ida Mae's fingernails cut into his wrist. Olin relaxed. She was of prime importance, keeping her safe and free from the claws of someone like Cyrus Morgan. "We'll be there."

The sheriff shook his head no. "Not you, Olin. Ida Mae. You're goin' to hafta trust me to take care of this. Olin, you can't be leanin' on the ways of the past to take care of things."

Olin swallowed hard. His stomach tightened into a ball.

"Can I be close by?"

"Yes, so long as Cyrus doesn't catch sight of you with Ida Mae." The sheriff turned to the rocking chair. "May I?"

"Yes. Please." Ida Mae stumbled as she stepped toward the sofa.

Olin reached out to steady her. "Ida Mae seems to think she might know how her signature could have appeared on that marriage certificate, if it is her signature."

"I'd like to hear it." The sheriff leaned back.

Ida Mae went on to explain how she had been signing several papers one day for the agreement with Cyrus to lease her parents' farm. "I don't recall signing anything but the lease, but I suppose it's possible. . . ."

"Am I correct in understanding that Cyrus told you he and Rosey had married?"

"Yes, sir."

Olin wrapped a protective arm around Ida Mae. This poor woman had been put in an elaborate trap. For what? Her property? "Sheriff, what made ye suspicious of Cyrus? I mean, that marriage certificate had me baffled."

"I'd been leaning that way for a while now. When he produced the certificate I was perplexed, but I knew about Rosey. As much as Cyrus is trying to hide it, he hasn't done a very good job. And then there's the gold mining he's been doing—"

"Gold mining?" Olin and Ida Mae asked in unison.

"I believe he found a nugget when he was working on rebuilding your farmhouse. I believe he thinks the farm has a rich supply. He just hasn't found it."

"Father and his friends churned that field over real well when gold was found on John Reed's farm back before I was born. The gold he found must have been the one small nugget Father kept as a reminder of how foolish a man could be if his heart isn't in the right place. It must have melted in the fire and hardened again."

"Possibly, but the reports I heard was he found the gold before your parents died. I have reason to believe Cyrus might have been responsible for the fire in your parents' house."

Olin held Ida Mae closer as her body shook.

"Are ye certain?" Olin wished the sheriff had never mentioned this tidbit if he had no facts to back it up.

"I'm sorry, Ida Mae. I don't mean no disrespect, but I'm very concerned about Cyrus being a real threat to more people in this community. I intend to look further into whether he's behind the fire, but for now, we need to clear your name and the fact that you are not married to the man. The false claim is enough to get him behind bars if you press charges. I'm hoping you will, miss."

Ida Mae sniffled her agreement. "Yes."

"Good. Now this is the hard part."

Can the situation get any harder than this? Olin wondered. He rubbed Ida Mae's upper arm and kissed her soft hair. "I love you," he whispered.

"Ida Mae, I want you to come with me and stay with my wife and me this evening."

"Why?" Olin squeaked.

"Precaution. I believe she's safe here, but let's not take any chances. Cyrus might be in a dangerous place, but at the moment he believes he has the upper hand. Let's keep it that way."

"All right." Ida Mae got up from the sofa. A cold chill swept over Olin's right arm and right side of his body. He prayed the only prayer he could for Ida Mae these days. *Dear God, please keep her safe.*

✎

Unable to contemplate the depth of Cyrus Morgan's greed, Ida Mae went over every detail the sheriff had told her. She even made him rehearse it again before she went to bed. Why would God allow the sins of a greedy man to take the lives of her parents? *Why, Lord?* she cried out in her morning prayers. She'd spent the night in a numb state, thinking and rethinking over the past couple years, ever since Cyrus Morgan entered her and her parents' lives.

The scripture reference that kept coming back to mind

was the one Olin and she had shared about being tested and refined in the Refiner's fire. She could understand how a metal worker would cling to that verse, yet now the same verse was wrapping itself as a golden ring around her heart, sometimes a wee bit too tightly, or so it seemed.

Would God allow the deaths of her parents in order to teach her more about her own relationship with God? Ida Mae shook. Oh, sure, she knew and understood there was sin in this world, and sin caused death, but for the first time she was seeing how much she'd been holding on to "Why me, Lord?" regarding the tragic events in her life instead of asking "How can I grow from this?"

Look at how much you've grown, she told herself, *how many precious gifts the Lord has given you since your parents died. You're a thriving businesswoman graced with a man who is not intimidated by your career or income.* It was remarkably true. Olin found her to be a woman he could call a companion. That wasn't to say she wouldn't mind being a helpmate to him and helping his business grow. The idea of simply taking care of a house and raising babies sounded mighty pleasing at the moment.

"Ida Mae!" Mrs. Thatcher called from behind the closed door. "It's just about time, dear."

"Thank you, I'll be out shortly."

Ida Mae stayed on her knees. "Father, please reveal to all the sins of Cyrus. Please release me from any legal obligations with him. And please don't allow it to be so that I'm his wife. Please, Lord, not that."

Taking in a deep pull of air, she lifted herself off the floor.

The door opened with a creak. Mrs. Thatcher smiled when Ida Mae entered the kitchen. "I made you a cup of tea and there's a leftover biscuit from breakfast. There's honey in the pot. Help yourself."

Ida Mae sat down, scraping the chair along the floor. "I'm sorry."

"Don't pay that no never mind. You just relax. John told me about what's been happening to you." Mrs. Thatcher wiped her hands on a towel and sat down across the table from her with a bowl of peaches and a small knife. "Today I'm making preserves. Yesterday I canned three dozen jars of peaches. By the time I'm done with this I won't want to see a peach again."

Ida Mae remembered life on the farm as a constant cycle of canning and harvesting food for the winter. "Are you drying any of the peaches?"

"Yes. I have a bushel out back, drying as we speak. John loves them in his porridge. I'm praying we don't get rain."

Finishing up her biscuit, Ida Mae wiped her hands on the linen napkin, then replaced it in her lap.

"I'll be happy to walk you over to John's office. He suggested you wear a scarf over your bonnet."

Fear wiggled around her neck muscles. Was her life really in danger? *Lord, keep me safe.*

❧

Olin sat in the saloon across the street from the sheriff's office. He had a perfect view. Cyrus Morgan had entered and five minutes later another man entered. More than likely, the justice of the peace. They hadn't been in there for more than five minutes when he spotted Rosey trying to peek into the jail. *What is she doing?*

Probably the same as me—watching, wondering, and waiting to see what final outcome the day will bring. Does she know? Is she a part of this? Truthfully, he hoped that Rosey was an innocent victim. If Cyrus had succeeded in this charade, Rosey might have been in grave danger, whether she was a part of it or not.

Two women approached the sheriff's office. A slit of a smile lifted his lips. He'd know that woman anywhere. How could every ounce of her be permanently attached to his brain in a few short months? "Lord, protect her," Olin mumbled into his sarsaparilla.

❧

Ida Mae kept her head bowed as she walked into Sheriff Thatcher's office. The three men sat around the sheriff's desk. "Yes, it was a fine day," Cyrus crooned.

"May I help you, Miss?" Sheriff Thatcher called out to her.

Ida Mae lifted her head and removed her bonnet and scarf.

"Ida Mae," Cyrus squeaked. He seemed to visibly pale in front of her.

"Elmer, is this the woman you married Cyrus to?"

"Can't say I've seen her before."

"Married me?" Ida Mae objected. "What are you talking about? I didn't marry Cyrus. Rosey Turner did. What's going on?" She looked at the sheriff, then turned to Cyrus. She placed her hands on her hips. "Cyrus?"

He pulled at his collar and squirmed in his chair.

"The gal I married Cyrus to has strawberry blond hair, kinda curly."

That fit Rosey's description. She narrowed her gaze on Cyrus once again.

Cyrus gathered his thoughts. "Ida Mae, please tell me you can remember our wedding day."

"Cyrus, we're not married, never have been and never will be. Where's Rosey?"

"How should I know? Honey, please sit and tell me where you've been. What happened? Did you fall off your horse?"

Cyrus's attempt to play the part of a doting husband failed miserably in Ida Mae's assessment. "Stop lying, Cyrus. Whatever your purpose, it is over. I've been safe with the Orrs. The sheriff has known how to find me all along. We hoped whoever was behind all my misfortune would show his hand in my absence. And I must say, you've done that. But what I don't understand is why. Why would you do this?" She wanted to scream, *Why did you kill my parents?* but it was too soon for such an accusation. The sheriff had more investigating to do. Everything she'd ever believed about Cyrus had changed forever.

"Is this your signature, Miss McAuley?"

The sheriff handed the document over to her. It felt foreign in her hands. She glanced down at the signature, then held the paper up to the light. Something didn't look right. "It looks very similar to my signature, but it doesn't flow the way I flow my letters together. Almost, but not quite." She'd been fully expecting to see her signature after the discussion she and Olin had back at the cottage. "Cyrus, why are you doing this?"

The door slammed against the wall. Rosey stood there with her hands on her hips. "You told the sheriff you married Ida Mae? You lyin'. . . Father was right. I shouldn't have married you."

"Rosey, hush."

"I will not hush!"

"That's the woman," the justice of the peace pointed out. "Cyrus, you're under arrest."

twenty-one

"Rumors and innuendos do not make it fact." The sheriff's words played through her mind over and over again. It had been three weeks since Cyrus was arrested, and still Ida Mae had more questions than answers.

Olin had moved his shop back into her father's smithy. Their marriage was pending, awaiting the outcome of the trial. There should be no question, but Cyrus was still standing by his statement that he had married Ida Mae. Olin and Ida Mae's relationship was blossoming even under the pressure. Ida Mae couldn't wait until the circuit judge would ride into town and hear their case. But until the sheriff had more proof that Cyrus set the fire to Ida Mae's parents' house, nothing further could be done on that charge.

Ida Mae prayed everyone would know what really happened once and for all. It had been hard enough knowing her parents had died in an accident. To think of them having been murdered bothered her in a way she'd never experienced before. In spite of, or perhaps because of, everything that had happened, her faith had grown tremendously over the summer.

"Good evening, Ida Mae." Olin stepped up beside her and gently squeezed her hand. She'd been waiting for him on the small front porch of the shop. She and Olin had set a couple of chairs out there so they could spend time with one another in public and yet have some privacy. "I missed ye."

"How was your meeting?"

"Good. I got the job."

"What job?" She knew full well which job. The one he couldn't speak to her about.

Olin captured her in his arms and whispered in her ear. The gentle heat of his breath caused her to melt like butter on a hot

165

biscuit. "I've been commissioned to design the plates for the first gold coins to be printed in Charlotte."

"Really? That's wonderful." She hugged him tighter. She knew he was an artist and did the finest tinwork she'd ever seen. Even the jeweler chose to sell some of Olin's products in his store. But to be granted such a secretive task. . . "How'd this happen?"

"Come sit down. Believe it or not, we have Cyrus and Percy to thank for this opportunity."

"What?" How could that be—she cut her thoughts off. One thing she'd learned over the past few months is that God works wonders out of the ashes of grief.

Olin sat down on one of the sitting chairs. Ida Mae sat down beside him. "If Percy hadn't complained to the sheriff about me, he wouldn't have taken the time to speak with me. Then when the unusual events began to happen around you, the sheriff again found me to be a trustworthy man. He recommended me to Mr. Bechtler, who was looking for a craftsman to design his gold dollar."

"Olin, I'm so proud of you." She reached out and held his hand.

"Thank ye. It means the world to me that you're pleased. My work with Mr. Bechtler should produce further sales of my tinware. Hopefully by next spring we can get married and I'll be able to provide for you."

"I received a letter today letting me know that my brothers will be coming to town in a few weeks. If they agree, I've decided to sell the land. I don't think I can step back into that house knowing what I know now about Cyrus."

Olin got up and knelt in front of her. "Honey, I know this has been a hard decision. Do ye think we should go to the house, first and see if it's still what ye want to do?"

"The house isn't the same, not after the fire. I'll miss the memories, but it's practical to sell the house and farm. You and I don't need it."

Olin smiled. "I'll see if Kyle will give me a hand building our house this winter so it will be ready for our wedding. Ye are still going to marry me?"

"Do you want to move into my parents' house?" she asked pensively.

"Honey, it can wait. We can wait. Ye and I have had a bumpy road to our love. I believe the extra time before marriage will be a blessing to us, a chance to really learn about one another."

But I want to marry you now. "Perhaps I should keep the house. We could marry sooner."

"Ida Mae, I'd marry ye today if we were settled on this legal proclamation, but I see this as another time of refinement. The time of waiting for the Refiner's gold to cool and harden, to become a permanent bar of precious metal. I can't wait to be able to purchase gold rings to wear on our fingers."

Lord, I love this man. He knows You so well. He teaches me daily to go deeper in my relationship with You. "Are you sure you want to wait?"

Olin chuckled and stood up. He stepped to the window and placed his hands on the sill. "Aye, I'm sure. The Lord has a design for our marriage. It's our choice to take the time and build a solid foundation."

And he couldn't be more right, Lord. "If that's what you want, I'm happy to go along with it. I love you, Olin, and I want to be your wife."

Between the beat of her heart and her last word, Olin closed the distance between them and held her close. "I love ye, Ida Mae, and I would be honored to be your husband."

epilogue

Ida Mae couldn't believe her wedding day had finally arrived. Her mind flickered over the past two years. The judge found Cyrus to be a fraud, and eventually the sheriff found the proof that Cyrus was responsible for her parents' deaths. It had been hard to believe that Cyrus's original plan was simply to marry Ida Mae and gain control of the farm. He had found a few small nuggets of gold on the farm before the fire. According to the facts, Ida Mae's father refused to force Ida Mae to marry Cyrus and told him the choice would be Ida Mae's. In a rage, he killed her father, and when her mother came to see what the matter was, he killed her, too. The fire was to cover the fact that they had been murdered. When her brothers arrived last fall, they decided to sell the property to Kyle Orr. They waived the first year's payment because the land was in such sad shape from all of Cyrus's gold mining attempts. Cyrus was hanged for the murder of her parents.

Mr. Bechtler's son, August, and nephew, Christopher, were opening their private mint and assay office. The miners were delighted. Olin's design for the coin had been acceptable, and he and Kyle finally finished the house.

"Ida Mae, are you ready?" Minnie ran into the room off the foyer where the minister liked to keep brides waiting until the time of the service. "Oh my, you're beautiful, Ida Mae. You did a real fine job on your dress."

"Thank you." She had opted for a fine silk she had bartered from Mrs. Farres six months ago.

"I still can't believe you're marryin' Olin. He's too perfect."

Ida Mac guffawed.

"What?"

"You. The first time you heard about him, you—"

"Don't you go fussin' about what I said then. I was hoodwinked. Percy is a real. . ."

Ida Mae's thoughts drifted back to the conversation she and Olin finally had about what happened on that fateful day when he had killed a man. Percy feared Olin would reveal that Percy himself had set up the fight in order to intimidate Gary Jones into releasing him from a gambling debt. It was Percy who had kept the rumors of Olin's guilt alive for so long, trying to avoid the inevitable embarrassment, not to mention the gambling debt. Once the truth came out, Olin had persuaded Percy to make restitution to the widows' fund at church. But the truth hadn't changed the past. Olin had been wrong and had lost control of his temper, costing a man his life. Today Percy would be sitting in a pew with the rest of the family. Ida Mae didn't anticipate them ever being close, but she didn't foresee any further trouble, either.

"Anyway," Minnie fussed, "I'm so glad you finally came to your senses and are marryin' this man."

Ida Mae smiled. If Minnie only knew how close she'd come a year ago. Then it would have been for all the wrong reasons. Today she stood in confidence of her love and Olin's love for her.

Uncle Ty knocked on the door. "Are ya ready, Ida Mae? It's time." He had agreed to give her away on behalf of their family. Her brothers couldn't attend, as it was harvest time.

"I'm ready." Ida Mae stepped out of the room as the piano played.

❧

Olin stood at the front of the church, his palms sweating. He wiped them on his trousers once again. One of the first gold coins struck from the Bechtlers' mint had been given to him as a wedding present. Olin knew they'd never spend it. It would be an honored and treasured gift, and he knew Ida Mae would feel the same.

A little over a year ago, he'd come to town sure of himself and confident it was time to come home. But just like the corduroy roads he had to mend along the great wagon road to get here from Pennsylvania, so was the relationship between him and Ida Mae. She was a beauty too lovely to be his. A gift from God he didn't deserve. Refined gold and as pure as silver. *Lord, help me remain worthy of her love.*

The notes on the piano began to ring out. Olin turned toward the doors at the back of the church. In walked his nephew with pillow in hand. He prayed the thread his sister sewed the rings on with was strong enough to hold the rings and yet loose enough for him and Ida Mae to pull them off at the right time in the ceremony. Then the twins marched down in their precious flower girl outfits, tossing petals on the floor. Olin couldn't wait to have children with Ida Mae.

Then she appeared. His mouth dried. His mind swam through the past sixteen months. It seemed like he'd always known her and yet, he really hadn't. The gentle sway of her hips as she came closer made him stiffen his knees so they wouldn't buckle.

She stood beside him. "Ye are beautiful," he whispered.

"Ye ain't so bad yourself," she replied with a wink.

Olin smiled. *Thank Ye, Lord.*

A Letter To Our Readers

Dear Reader:

In order that we might better contribute to your reading enjoyment, we would appreciate your taking a few minutes to respond to the following questions. We welcome your comments and read each form and letter we receive. When completed, please return to the following:

Fiction Editor
Heartsong Presents
PO Box 719
Uhrichsville, Ohio 44683

1. Did you enjoy reading *Corduroy Road to Love* by Lynn A. Coleman?
   ❑ Very much! I would like to see more books by this author!
   ❑ Moderately. I would have enjoyed it more if

   _____

   _____

   _____

2. Are you a member of **Heartsong Presents**? ❑ Yes ❑ No
   If no, where did you purchase this book? _____

   _____

3. How would you rate, on a scale from 1 (poor) to 5 (superior), the cover design? _____

4. On a scale from 1 (poor) to 10 (superior), please rate the following elements.

   ____ Heroine   ____ Plot
   ____ Hero   ____ Inspirational theme
   ____ Setting   ____ Secondary characters

5. These characters were special because? _____

_____

_____

6. How has this book inspired your life? _____

_____

_____

7. What settings would you like to see covered in future
   Heartsong Presents books? _____

_____

_____

8. What are some inspirational themes you would like to see
   treated in future books? _____

_____

_____

9. Would you be interested in reading other **Heartsong
   Presents** titles? ❏ Yes ❏ No

10. Please check your age range:
    ❏ Under 18   ❏ 18-24
    ❏ 25-34   ❏ 35-45
    ❏ 46-55   ❏ Over 55

Name _____

Occupation _____

Address _____

City, State, Zip _____

CALIFORNIA BRIDES

Heart♥ng

Presents